It was all Callie had ever dreamed of and all she had ever wanted, making love with Sage. It was slow and beautiful and sensuous. It was the touch of sensitive fingers and a dewy rain of delicate kisses; then it was a flame of passion that blotted out reason, and it was the gentle lowering of that inferno to a basking glow.

Truths and half truths, secrets and evasions, who was wrong and who was right, none of it mattered as Callie and Sage opened all for another and became one. Together they sought, together they found, and together they reached the end of that long and empty journey. It felt like coming home....

Dear Reader,

We're so proud to bring you Harlequin
Intrigue. These books blend adventure and
excitement with the compelling love stories
you've come to associate with Harlequin.

This series is unique; it combines contem-
porary themes with the fast-paced action
of a good old-fashioned page turner.
You'll identify with these realistic heroines
and their daring spirit as they seek the
answers, flirting with both danger and
passion along the way.

We hope you'll enjoy these new books,
and look forward to your comments
and suggestions.

The Editors
Harlequin Intrigue
919 Third Avenue
New York, N.Y. 10022

THE KEY
REBECCA FLANDERS

Harlequin Books

TORONTO • NEW YORK • LONDON
AMSTERDAM • PARIS • SYDNEY • HAMBURG
STOCKHOLM • ATHENS • TOKYO • MILAN

Harlequin Intrigue edition published August 1984

ISBN 0-373-22001-4

Chapter One

When Callie left the apartment, she suspected she was incorrectly dressed. The moment she stepped on campus she was sure of it.

The last time Callie had been on a university campus the fashion had been faded jeans and chambray shirts, gold chains and white jackets worn without a shirt. Students drove Volkswagens with bumper stickers that said *May The Force Be With You* and John Denver regaled the virtues of a natural high by day, while John Travolta gave a new meaning to the word disco by night.

The modern-day student parking lot was filled with Mazdas, Z-28s, and Firebirds. Bumper stickers were out, alligator shirts were in. So were oxfords, plaid skirts, knee socks and cardigans tied around the neck. Callie's brown linen suit with its short, cap-sleeved jacket and prim white blouse was definitely out. So were her worn Moroccan leather sandals with their comfortable one-inch heels.

Callie Lester felt very old, awkward and—what was most unusual for her—extremely unsure of herself. During her career as an interpreter, she had been around the world twice, crossed the International Dateline so often she had stopped counting, and was intimately familiar with every major airport in the world and a few that were not even on the map. The freeways of America, the twisting cobbled streets of Europe, the mountain trails of South America, even the jungles of Africa were no problem; she could find her way with ease through the back alleys and major thoroughfares of any industrial city in the world. But on a modern university campus in Middle America she was completely lost.

Callie was twenty-nine years old and felt twice that age. Worse, she felt as though every face she passed knew it and registered it with a curious look...what was she doing here, anyway? Callie wished she could answer that question herself.

What she did not know was that on first glance, and even second, there was nothing about her physical appearance to indicate she was any older than the students who mingled around her and only last year had been high school seniors. Her dark hair with its natural waves was not cut in the latest style, to be sure, but it framed a face that was innately youthful before it fell in wispy curls around her collar. Her high cheekbones emphasized eyes that were already wide and innocently observant and darkly framed with long, almost obscenely luxurious lashes. Her eyebrows needed little shaping or darkening, but followed a natural arch that, unfortunately, was too often disguised by the thick bangs that fell over her forehead.

The golden tan that still lingered from her time abroad gave her skin an apricot sheen that other women who had spent their summers baking at some pool, only to have their tans fade with the first falling leaf, could only envy. Her mouth, which Callie had always considered her worst feature, was the perfect bow shape of a young child's. The lower lip was fuller than the upper, which gave her a sometimes sultry, sometimes sullen look that Callie hated. She was constantly being accused of pouting when she was in fact doing nothing of the sort, and what other people considered an endearing feature Callie only thought of as a nuisance.

Though she stood five-five in stocking feet, her frame was small and her figure slight. Callie had never been able to settle down anywhere long enough to get fat. But then, she had never worn jogging shorts or a miniskirt or even a tennis dress, and the opportunities to show off her figure, if she had so desired, had escaped her. Callie Lester was a businesswoman through and through, and today she felt very out of place.

Of course, Callie had heard of the preppy look and the Datsun 280ZX, but none of these trends had yet touched the inner sanctum of a corporate headquarters building where she worked in Buenos Aires. In fact the only hint Callie had had of American trends for the past two years had been via mail-order catalogs that were already a year out of date by the time she received them. Fashion had not exactly been a high priority with Callie in her most recent occupation. Mosquitoes, heat, and international finance had pretty much taken precedence over more urbane concerns.

Some people thought Callie was lucky. She had in the past eight years lived in three foreign countries and touched ground at least once in almost every other nation in the world, and she had been paid enormously for the privilege. Even her last employer, who had done nothing but complain about the condition of his stomach, the heat, the isolation, and the cultural loneliness the whole two years they were in South America, did not understand why she would want to give up such a promising career to get a second master's degree at her age. Her skills as an interpreter were in great demand; her fluency in culture and protocol were as valuable to the international businessman as her mastery of language. Callie could pick and choose her own assignments. She should be the teacher, Augustus Jordan had argued as he popped one antacid pill after the other, not the student; furthermore, there wasn't a woman alive who wouldn't fight for a job like hers, filled with excitement, adventure, unlimited travel and almost unlimited salary. What did she have to complain about? How could she improve upon perfection?

Callie could not explain to Augustus Jordan the real reason she wanted to go back to school, so she merely reiterated the fact that her education was incomplete if she expected to excel in her chosen profession. Fluency in the Romance languages was no longer enough to be successful. She needed to achieve a level of competence in Russian, Japanese.

and Arabic at the very least if she intended to further her career...and she was not exactly certain that was what she intended to do. She knew she was tired of wandering and wanted to settle down. And Callie wanted to do it within the borders of the continental United States. She was also tired of only repeating the words of others; sometimes she yearned to be the one who created the words, who made the decisions, who established policy. Perhaps what Callie had in mind, vaguely if at all, was a job at the UN or in the State Department, and for either of those positions she needed a degree in something other than languages.

Callie always tried to justify decisions that she knew were made entirely without the advantage of logic, but this time she was not even having much luck convincing herself. This was an impulsive move, like so many in her life, based not on reason but on emotion—a hunch, intuition, or a vague hope—and, like so many others, it was motivated by one thing and one thing only. That she could not explain to Augustus Jordan or anyone else. She wasn't entirely sure she could even explain it sufficiently to herself.

But despite all else, Callie Lester was an American and she wanted to go home. She wanted to see first-run movies and late-model cars; she wanted popcorn and fudge ripple ice cream; she wanted to know what Halston and Lauren were doing this season; and she wanted to see a baseball game that was not four weeks old and sub-titled. She did not know whether she would ever achieve the security of her own permanent office somewhere in Washington, D.C., and was not even sure how much she cared. She was just glad to be home.

So for the first three weeks on American soil, Callie had wandered around like a starstruck tourist, counting the windows on skyscrapers, attending boat shows and rock concerts, window shopping, and taking two-hour bubble baths. She wanted to go to New York; she wanted to cross the Continental Divide; she wanted to buy a car and spend the summer discovering rural America. Instead she took a short-term lease on a furnished apartment in Dallas, which was the first major stop the plane from Buenos Aires made, and watched television with endless fascination twelve hours a day. She bought a stereo and so many record albums that she had not yet played them all. One morning she spent an entire hour simply standing in front of the post office, watching the flag wave against a cobalt-blue sky. She saw every movie in town, read every gossip magazine on the stands, and tried every variety of frozen dinner in the market. Some people missed hot dogs and hamburgers; Callie missed Sara Lee. Two years were gone from her life and she frantically tried to cram them into a few weeks, but she knew all along she was just marking time.

Finally she could stand it no longer and she put in a long-distance call to Jerry Sloane. She tried not to let herself hope for too much, and Jerry, in turn, urged her not to be too encouraged. But it was that phone call which, four months later, had resulted in

Callie Lester's presence on a midwestern university campus seeking a degree in Mideastern Affairs—out of date, out of touch, and out of style.

Sometimes Callie dreamed that she was wandering an empty, foggy street, cold and alone. Her muscles ached, her mind was dull, she was exhausted. She only wanted to go home. Home was a shingled cottage on a cul-de-sac, surrounded by a white picket fence laden with roses and climbing wisteria. The fragrance of wood smoke wisped from the chimney and every window glowed with yellow warmth. Inside, hardwood floors gleamed with beeswax and bright rag rugs splashed mirrors of color on their surfaces. There were pine tables and blue chintz, bone china, and book-lined walls. There was a big bed upstairs with a down comforter and a deep-cushioned rocking chair by the window. Inside there was a crackling fire and the smell of good things from the kitchen. Inside there were people who loved her.

In the dream she climbed three stone steps to the heavy oak door, and with each step fatigue dropped from her and excitement built. In a few moments she would be inside where it was safe and warm. Any moment now she would be home.

She turned the knob on the sturdy door—a door built for security, keeping the good things inside and unwelcome intruders out. But the door wouldn't open. It was locked, and Callie had lost the key.

Maybe, she thought as she made her way with some perplexity through the usual first-day confu-

sion of the otherwise orderly campus, Jerry Sloane
had given her that key. Or maybe this was just another wild-goose chase, another knot in the tangled
skein of yarn that was Callie Lester's life. . . .

"Don't, for heaven's sake, go doing anything
foolish, Callie," Jerry had insisted, exasperated.
"This could mean nothing—nothing! I mean, I've
been in this business for ten years and I've had some
slim leads, but this has got to take the cake. I
wouldn't have told you at all, but I knew you'd
make my life miserable until you got something out
of me... And now look what you're doing. You're
going to go flying off on a crazy tangent and make
your own life miserable. . ."

"Better me than you, huh?" Callie had grinned
irrepressibly, but Jerry would not be teased.

"It's probably not the man you're looking for,"
he told her soberly. "And even if he was there once,
what makes you think he'd still be there, just hanging around waiting for someone to find him. . . ?
Men like that don't stay put long, Callie. You've
got to know that—they can't afford to."

Then Callie had to get serious. She knew everything Jerry was saying was true; they had been
through it before off and on for the past eight
years. And she knew he was right. She could not—
and she would not—let her life be governed by the
pursuit of a man who had disappeared off the face
of the earth twenty years ago. She had her head
straight about that. And so she told Jerry truthfully
that she was not making plans based solely on the
scanty information he had given her but she had to

try to solve her personal mystery. Besides, she had been thinking for a long time about going back to college. One advantage of living on the outskirts of civilization for years at a time was that there was no opportunity to spend money, so she had saved enough to take a sabbatical. It was true she needed the time to sort out her life and plan new career directions. Jerry had just made it a little easier to choose the way, that was all.

But today, standing in the middle of a network of crisscrossing white sidewalks and pristine green lawns, jostled by preppy freshmen who were just as perplexed as she was, Callie had to give serious consideration to the possibility that she had made a mistake. She was too old for this—too old and maybe too wise. Going back to school at age twenty-nine... what could she possibly expect to have in common with these fresh-faced youngsters who had not yet even taken the first step on the road to life? Oh, sure, she had heard of adult education, but night classes on How to Improve Your Vocabulary and Career Orientation were quite different from moving into the mainstream of university life, football games, cheerleaders, and student rallies....

So who said anything about football games? Or the other students, for that matter. Callie was taking day classes full-time for one reason: to complete her education in the fastest and most economical way. A profession like hers, even if she could find a position that did not take her out of the country, required that she be on call twenty-four hours a day, and she could hardly expect to make any progress at all if she was only free to catch an odd class once or twice a month. The only practical thing to do was take the time off and devote herself to full-time study.

And that was another thing. Callie had saved money, it was true, but was it really practical to blow her whole life's savings on one enterprise that may or may not pay off in the future? Suppose by the time she completed her education the market for her talent had dried up? She did not know how long she might be out of work. As it was, she was going to have to find a roommate to share the expenses of living off campus or she would never be able to afford to complete her planned course of study. And what if, midway through, she decided she needed to take extra courses or even go for a PhD? Self-improvement did not come cheap these days.

She was self-conscious and uncertain, and the thought of walking into a classroom filled with twenty-year-olds gave her a queasy feeling in the pit of her stomach. She did not belong here. She did not even know where she was.

Pursuant to that problem, Callie glanced again at the registration slip in her hand and then toward the low sand-colored building before her. "Languages" was carved in block letters across the top, and she guessed that was the place she was supposed to be. She started up the steps.

Callie was still trying to decipher the computer printout of her registration slip to determine which room number was assigned to which class and at what time; she was not really watching where she was going, but it was doubtful anything she could have done would have prevented the collision. A young man came bounding up the steps three at a time, caught his elbow on the stack of books she was carrying, sent Callie whirling around and the books flying.

With an exclamation of dismay, Callie teetered on the edge of the step for a frantic moment, then he caught her arm and jerked her upright. "Sorry!" he exclaimed and bent quickly to salvage her books before they were trampled by other hurried feet.

"It's all right; I guess I was—"

She bent down to help him, but he had already gathered her books and the only thing that detained him was one last lingering look at her calves, bare and shapely beneath the hem of her skirt. Callie was both amused and flattered. A shaggy-haired blond with impish eyes and an endearing grin, he couldn't have been more than twenty. Had she passed the first test of peer-group acceptance?

He straightened up with that open, appreciative grin sweeping her again from bottom to top, and he said, "My own technique for meeting women. It's a little rough around the edges, but it works every time." He handed her books back to her. "I'm Brad Johnson. Where're you headed?"

It was impossible to be offended by a sparkle that mischievous, a face that innocent. Callie laughed and maneuvered her books to the other arm to show him her registration slip. "Here, I think. I'm not really sure."

He glanced at the paper. "Well, Callie Lester..." he read from the top, and then winked at her. "You're in luck. Just follow me."

She did not have to actually follow him, as he shifted the weight of his own books to his other hip and cupped her elbow lightly with his hand. Callie did not mind the intimacy—all part of the new freedom of today's youth, she supposed. And it was good to have a friend.

The building was modern and efficient, the classroom into which Brad led her a model of technology and design. Instead of desks there were computer terminals, instead of walls there were sunshielded windows, instead of a blackboard there was a video screen. The room was filled to capacity with students, some of whom were already getting adventurous with the terminals at their seats. Callie had had no idea so many people would be interested in taking Russian.

"Wow," she murmured, sliding behind the console next to Brad. "Some set up, huh?" She curiously fingered the keyboard in front of her. "What do you suppose all this is for?"

Brad shot her an amused look. "How else are you going to learn BASIC? This is really kid's stuff," he confided, leaning a little closer as he absently switched on the machine. The television screen glowed grayly with a pleasant hum as the terminal came to life. "But I needed the course credit. What about you? Are you a novice?"

"Not exactly," Callie answered, frowning a little. She was beginning to have a definite feeling something was wrong.

"These are limited-system terminals," Brad observed, competently inserting a floppy disk into the computer and producing a quick display of flashing screens with the deft movements of his fingers across the keyboard. "No good for anything but practice." And he grinned. "Too bad, huh? We could have some fun with old Rathbone if we could plug into his system."

Callie was becoming more and more uneasy. She glanced around at the filled classroom and at the skinny, red-haired gentleman who was strolling to the front. "Who is Rathbone?"

Brad nodded toward the man at the front of the room who was calling for attention by sharply rapping the frame of his glasses against one of the computer terminals.

"Brad," Callie whispered, now definitely disturbed. "What class is this?"

He looked at her, puzzled. "BASIC Programming. What did you think it was?"

Callie looked in dismay at her registration slip. "Russian!"

The murmuring had ceased, and Brad barely caught a whoop of laughter that would have made them both the center of unwelcome attention. Mr. Rathbone began to address the class in a dry monotone that was completely lost on Callie's frantically racing brain. Just her luck! First day of class and she had to have a schedule mix-up. As though she weren't feeling awkward enough, now she was going to have to get up and walk out of a class well in progress, that was assuming she could even figure out where she was supposed to go from here. . .

Brad had taken her registration slip from her and was busily punching in keys on the computer. "What is a computer programming class doing in the Languages building?" Callie wailed under her breath, and then looked at him in alarm. "This *is* Languages, isn't it?"

Brad grinned. "BASIC is a language," he informed her, and he pointed to a screen of numbers that made no sense to her whatsoever. "So the computer assigned it the same prefix as any other language course, only someone punched in the wrong digit on your card."

"You mean I'm registered for this class?" she moaned, gray eyes darkening in despair.

"Is there a problem over here?" Dr. Rathbone had directed his dry, disinterested monotone toward them, and Callie jumped guiltily, her cheeks reddening.

"I—I seem to be in the wrong place. . ." she stammered.

Brad was quickly punching out more numbers. "Basic Russian—room 217," he hissed, shoving her card back to her. "Don't try to explain—just get out of here before this machine swallows you whole."

Callie could barely restrain a nervous giggle along with her look of sheer gratitude as she fumbled to get her books together. Dr. Rathbone was glaring at her and she spared him a glance of apology as she stood. "Sorry," she mumbled. "I know where I'm supposed to be now."

"Then, pray, be there," the professor returned expressionlessly, and Callie scooted past him, trying to make herself invisible.

"Too bad," she heard Brad murmur just before the door was firmly closed behind her.

Chapter Two

This was definitely not the way to start a new and daring enterprise. Callie's palms were sweaty and she felt hot all over with embarrassment as she wandered down the labyrinth of nearly deserted halls, only hoping Brad had been right about the new room number. Now she had to walk into another strange classroom filled with people and present herself to another hostile professor. . .

She paused for just a second outside the closed door that was marked 217, firmly gathering her courage. At least in this room she would recognize the language being spoken. . .

Callie opened the door quietly and slipped inside, glancing neither right nor left, and made her way directly for the first available chair. Fortunately— or not so fortunately, perhaps—the closest empty chair was in the first row, right in front of the professor's desk. The professor himself, as seen from the corner of her eye, was perched on the edge of the desk, swinging one denim-clad leg in a lazy, circular motion before him, and did not let her entrance disturb the course of his speech. "In order to understand the roots of the language," he was saying, his tone easy and forthright, "we're going to have to understand the Russian people, the land, the culture. How did the language evolve to serve a people as unique as the Russians? How do they think? How do they act? What makes their society so fundamentally different from our own?"

Callie was breathing a sigh of relief as she sank unobstructively into her chair, thinking that if her tardy entrance had not gone unnoticed, it had at least gone unremarked. Time enough after class to straighten out the mess with her professor and the computer in the registration office. Right now all she wanted to do was remain anonymous.

And just when she was starting to relax in safety, the professor continued casually, "For example, if we were in Russia today and a young lady strolled into my class ten minutes late, she would in most likelihood be shot..." Heads turned and titters erupted as he got up and moved easily toward Callie's desk, and her humiliation was complete. She refused to raise her eyes to him. She was seething with anger and embarrassment and all she saw was a pair of lean masculine legs snugly encased in denim approaching her at a disturbingly lanky gait, then a slim brown hand coming down to cover the registration slip that rested on top of her books. His hand lingered there for just a moment, as though waiting for her to acknowledge his presence, and Callie fought the urge to let the point of her sandal make contact with his shin. That was all she needed, a smart-aleck instructor who probably knew less about the language than she did... This was a mistake, the whole thing. A big mistake.

"...or exiled to Siberia at least." He did not let the renewed snickers interrupt his lecture, and Callie cautiously unclenched her muscles as he merely picked up her registration slip and turned back toward his desk. "That's what most of you think, isn't it? Well, unfortunately, we all have some misconceptions about a culture which is about as different from ours as any could be. So for your first assignment you're going to read *The Russians* by Leo Ruse. It's eight hundred twenty pages long and I expect it finished by next Thursday. But don't worry, I'm giving you a break—it's in English."

There was another spattering of laughter mixed in with a few groans, and Callie became aware that there was a relaxed atmosphere in this classroom, which had been missing in the other. The students seemed to like this impudent cowboy, whoever he was.

Curiosity mingled with an innate pride refused to let her hide from him any longer. Callie lifted her eyes and stared at him boldly, and she began to understand how he had been able to establish such a quick rapport with his students.

Callie couldn't help thinking about the last movie she had seen before leaving for Argentina, that classic of old-time heroism and adventure that had won the hearts of America during her last summer in the States. This man brought it back as though it were yesterday. Indiana Jones was her first objective summary of the figure who lounged casually against his desk before her. All he needs is a battered cowboy hat and a bullwhip and he could be off to the wilds of Egypt in search of the Lost Ark...

He was probably no more than six feet tall, but his slim build and long legs gave the impression that he was much taller—almost rangy. His hair was dark brown, loosely curly and quite unruly, so lightly sprinkled with gray that the effect was more sun-kissed than salt-and-pepper. His face was unusually shaped—high forehead and cheekbones, perfectly square chin, and a natural groove along the side of his left cheek that gave him a rugged look...or perhaps it was a secretly amused look. Callie could not decide which. The deep cleft above his lips drew attention to a sensuous mouth that had a tendency to curve downward with wry humor. Yes, she decided, he was definitely a man who could always find something to amuse him, either in himself or others, and it was that easy-going attitude that permeated his entire character and made itself so quickly known to his students.

He was wearing a cordovan leather jacket, the zip-up, waist-length style, open over a camel V-neck sweater. A few curling brown hairs were visible at the plunge of that sweater and the only word for that was sexy. No wonder he had the women in the class mesmerized. Between the partially exposed chest and those jeans... She had already had quite a sufficient view of the parts of his anatomy covered by the jeans, so Callie directed her attention to his feet, which she was surprised to notice were encased in rugged motorcycle boots. That explained as well as anything else the almost palpable respect he received from the male students. A real man's man, off to save the world for democracy or the lady in distress from the black-bearded villain... He even held the pointer as though it were a whip handle, absently tapping it against one palm while he spoke, testing the leather, and any moment now it would snap out to capture a desperado's gun or wrap around the neck of some poor unsuspecting international spy...

He carried himself with the innate confidence of a man surprised by nothing, aware of everything, born with experience and comfortable with it. He walked in silent rolling strides around the classroom, every movement graceful and uncalculated but exuding power and a deep level of sensual magnetism. Muscles relaxed, head back, hands in pockets, he looked as though he would be more at home at a beach party or barbecue than in a formal classroom—he looked, in fact, as though he would prefer to be anywhere but in a formal classroom—yet there was that undercurrent of alertness, of sharp observation and keen assessment about him that Callie found somewhat disturbing.

It was nothing she could put her finger on, nothing even that she could put into words, but one of the most valuable things she had acquired in her profession was the ability to interpret the nuances behind the words, to assess character accurately, and to make judgments based often on no more than gut instinct. Something told her that this man had known danger. Callie once had had the singularly impressive experience of interpreting for a Brazilian oil millionaire who was considering entering into negotiation with the company she worked for. Later he had been discovered in a plan to overthrow the government. That oil tycoon had exuded the same sort of authority and shrewdness as did the professor who paced the room before her, and he had given her exactly the same uneasy feeling... As though he were not entirely what he appeared to be.

Or perhaps it was simply Callie's imagination working overtime again.

Whatever it was, he certainly carried it off well. If there was an aura of danger or intrigue about him, it was the kind that naturally affected women on the animal level, arousing an excitement or a fascination within them for which there was no logical explanation. Witness the success of Indiana Jones. Or maybe it was no more than the tight jeans.

Once more, on an impulse, Callie let her eyes wander over those distinctly shaped legs. Lean, but not skinny. Certainly not heavy. Her eyes moved in a leisurely, almost casual fashion over the bleached-out rounds of his knees, upward to taut thighs, and then because she simply couldn't help it—because the area was so well defined—she let her eyes rest on the faded denim that strained across his crotch.

Five seconds, no more, and then Callie became aware that he had stopped speaking. An awful feeling of certainty overwhelmed her even before she jerked her eyes upwards to meet sparks of mirth dancing from the navy blue ones of the man who had been watching her watching him...eyes filled with acknowledgment and mischief and a secret truth that made her want to sink through the floor with embarrassment.

He took two easy steps toward her and stopped before her desk, feet planted casually apart, hands thrust into his front pockets so that the material was stretched even tighter across the part of his anatomy at which now she desperately refused to look. "What do you think?" he asked her pleasantly in Russian.

The attention of the entire room was focused on the interchange and Callie felt certain they were all aware of exactly what had prompted it. She had to remind herself rather desperately that no one could have really been aware that she was staring at him except the object of her scrutinization himself and that in a class of Basic Russian no one would understand what he said. She could feel her heart thumping and her cheeks scorching and she thought how ridiculous it was: she had dealt with ambassadors and presidents and the men who rule the industries of the world, and never once had her cool aplomb deserted her in a social or business situation. Yet one small-town university instructor had in less than fifteen minutes destroyed her composure, rattled her nerves, and humiliated her twice before a roomful of people.

Callie lifted her chin and met his eyes boldly. She refused to succumb to this. She was Callie Lester, international traveler and successful career woman; Callie Lester, who should be the teacher and not the student; Callie Lester, in charge of her own destiny. She could handle this impudent range-roamer. She could handle anything.

"There is room for improvement," she informed him just as pleasantly and in the same language.

Callie surprised herself as much as she did him. Her knowledge of Russian was scanty at best—thus the refresher course—and she had not practiced it in years. She was both stunned and enormously pleased that the words came so easily to her lips, and her delight was only increased by the quick amazement in his eyes...just before he burst into uproarious laughter.

White teeth flashing, head thrown back, eyes snapping rakishly, his laugh was full bodied and ringing, and in other circumstances it would have been a beautiful, soul-lifting sound. It made Callie clench her teeth and restrain the urge to throw her textbook in his face.

Sobering only slightly as he turned back to his desk, his eyes still snapping with outrageous amusement, he tossed over his shoulder some comment in Russian she did not understand. She was positive it was lewd. Oh, what a mistake this had been. She had no business here in a room filled with people barely out of their teens, taking a course she really didn't need, making herself the target for harassment by a ridiculously sexy Russian professor... What was she trying to prove, anyway? And what would he do next—interpret for the whole class the words that had just passed between them and the reason for them?

But to her very great relief, he simply turned to the blackboard and began scrawling the elements of the Russian alphabet across it. He had terrible handwriting, but a rather attractive backside. Furious with herself for the observation and for the renewed stain of color in her cheeks that would be sure to earn her another amused look at the very least if he should turn unexpectedly around, Callie opened her notebook and began to meticulously copy the abstract scratchings he made on the board.

For another fifteen minutes the class passed uneventfully, and Callie lost her nervousness in the effort to follow his explanation of the origins of the Russian alphabet. She was only conversational in Russian, and even that left much to be desired. She had never learned to read or write the language and was only now beginning to see what a complex task she had set before herself. Was it really worth it? How could her head possibly hold all of this new material—all of it diametrically opposed to anything she had ever learned before—and possibly have any room left over to concentrate on anything else? She had been out of school too long. She wasn't going to make it.

Then when she had reached the very depths of her befuddlement and given up both on trying to understand his speech and trying to follow his aimless wandering course around the room, Callie saw the impudent professor alter his course and approach her. He made a deliberate circle around her desk, not a single change of tone or a pause in the flow of his lecture indicating that he was interested in anything other than the origins of the alphabet. As he walked he craned his neck to get the best possible view of her crossed legs from every angle, inspecting them and examining them, and finally lifting an eyebrow and nodding his head slightly in approval. Callie heard the restless movements of repressed laughter behind her, and she lifted her eyes to his in cold challenge. Once more she met only bland amusement in his, and he turned casually back to his desk with some reminder about the assignment due Thursday.

That was when Callie knew without a doubt that this was not going to work. Not at all.

When the class was dismissed, she gathered up her books and prepared to beat a hasty retreat. She should have known it would not be that easy.

"Miss Lester," drawled the by now all-too-familiar voice behind her. "Would you mind staying after class for a few minutes?"

Callie, who was now only two feet away from the door, gritted her teeth and swore silently to herself. She considered for a moment walking on as though she had not heard him, but Callie had never been the type to put off an unpleasant chore. She would have to face him sooner or later, if for no other reason than to retrieve her registration slip.

Callie turned slowly and walked on leaden feet back to his desk. With every step her heartbeat quickened. Nerves, she thought. Nothing at all to do with that sheer magnetism that radiated from every muscle as he leaned back in his chair, one long arm stretched across the desk to scribble notes on a paper before him, head tilted so that it caught the sunlight from the opposite window and profiled his face in angular shadows. Callie stood there as the room slowly emptied, watching the motes of dust caught in the splash of sunlight that fell across his desk, watching the competent, slim-fingered hand move the pen across paper, sensing the fragrance of leather and chalk, and all the while he ignored her. Obviously this was to be a private conversation. Why did that realization make her stomach muscles tighten? She felt like a naughty pupil being detained after school...which, she supposed, she was. Worse, she felt like a fifteen-year-old alone for the first time with the star quarterback—the fluttering pulses, the dry throat, the sweaty palms—and that irritated her. She was letting this entire campus routine get to her. Grow up, she scolded herself in annoyance. Remember who you are. This man can't be more than five years older than you are. Let's get a perspective on this thing...

The room was empty, the voices from the hallway grew ever more muted. The silence enfolded them like a blanket, and Callie waited, her nerves on edge, her patience wearing thin. Five more seconds, she thought, and then he looked up.

The sunlight sparked in his eyes and outlined flecks of cerulean there; his smile was lazy and relaxed and far too intimate. He stretched out his long legs and leaned back in the chair, balancing his fingertips over the ballpoint pen like a tent with the pen the center stake. And he drawled, "You're a spy, right? Dean Winslow sent you to disrupt my class, wreck my concentration, and play absolute hell with my body chemistry.''

With a great effort Callie managed to subdue a new rush of color. She lifted her chin and said stiffly, ''I'm sure I don't know what you mean. I—''

He picked up her registration slip and glanced at it casually. The leather jacket made crinkling sounds as he moved. ''You don't belong here,'' he said.

''I can explain that—''

''You obviously already speak Russian,'' he interrupted implacably, and beyond the mild curiosity on his face there was something else—mockery or a subtle challenge. This man had a face that could too easily disguise his motivations, and Callie did not like that at all. ''Why would a person already fluent in the language want to take a course in Basic Russian?''

Callie took a deep breath, trying not to glare at him. She had read *Winning Through Intimidation*, too, and she was not about to succumb to such practiced techniques. A power play, that was all it was. He was getting back at her for something— coming in late, the staring incident, or maybe just on general principles—by putting her in a submissive position to his authority. He was *trying* to make her feel like a naughty child. It wasn't going to work.

''If you would only listen for a moment,'' she told him deliberately, meeting him stare-for-stare, ''instead of talking while I'm talking, I will be glad to explain it to you.''

The slight incline of his head was accompanied by a quirk of the eyebrow that could have disguised amusement, and he settled back with an air of benevolent interest. Callie took another breath. "In the first place," she explained patiently, "the reason my registration slip is wrong is because of a computer foul-up. I am registered for this class—or at least I'm supposed to be. In the second place, I'm taking the beginning course because I need it. I don't read or write the language at all and I can only speak it very sparingly."

"How well do you speak the language?" he asked in Russian.

"Well enough to hold a general conversation," she replied haltingly in the same language, fumbling for the words. "Sometimes."

"Why do you want to improve?"

He was testing her conversational ability, and Callie struggled for the right reply in Russian. She knew her accent was terrible. "It's been many years since I spoke Russian," she managed. "I have lost much of the small skill I might once have had."

"Where did you originally learn?"

"From a friend," she replied, but that was not strictly true. She had taken a crash course from a Russian cab driver while she was living in New York in preparation for a two day visit to Moscow with the vice-president of the firm for which she was working at the time. That had been five years ago and she had realized even then that crash courses were not the way to further her career. Callie had been terrified the entire time that she would make some terrible faux pas in interpretation that would land both her and her boss in prison and possibly start a war. She had never been back to the Soviet Union—the experience was simply too nerve-racking—but she had occasionally been called upon to translate simple telephone conversations or to be present at a meeting where English was spoken as a second language by Russian participants. Fortunately on all those occasions she had managed to bumble her way through, and when a real problem arose she had always been able to find a second language—French, usually—in which they could communicate more easily. But she knew that if she were to reform her career around the highly exclusive—hopefully stateside—jobs that were available for only the most skilled interpreters, she could not afford to take chances like that any more.

The interest in his eyes appeared to be genuine, and he spoke with ease, as though they were truly conducting a casual conversation—in Russian. "A friend? How did that come about?"

Callie sighed, growing impatient. It was really too complicated a story to explain, especially in an unfamiliar language, and all she really wanted to do was get on with the business of assigning herself to the right class. She merely shrugged.

"Did you understand the question?" he inquired.

"I understood."

"Do you know how to answer it?"

"Yes."

"Then why don't you?"

"Because I don't think it's relevant," she replied firmly, using up the last of her expertise.

He did not seem to be offended. He merely sat there, lounging in his chair with one long forefinger resting against his temple, watching her thoughtfully. Callie wished suddenly and very intensely that her brown suit was not so out of style, so tacky, and so unattractive. She wished she had taken the curling iron to her hair this morning as she had intended to, instead of spending twenty minutes studying the map of the campus and trying to figure out the most efficient way to get from one building to another. She could feel her dark brown tresses hanging limply against her neck and strands of her bangs wilting down over her eyelashes, tickling every time she blinked. She wondered if she had chewed all her lipstick off.

He straightened up, the air of reverie that had been briefly upon him immediately dispersing, and began to speak to her easily and rapidly in Russian. She caught something about schedules and courses but beyond that she was lost. Before he had been speaking carefully and distinctly, as a teacher would to a student; now he lapsed into easy, heavily dialected conversation as though he had forgotten that English was his first language. Callie was amazed, and it showed on her face.

He stopped and grinned. "Sorry," he said in English, "I forget sometimes. Did you catch any of that?"

Callie shook her head slowly, burning to know where and how he had learned to speak so well. "Not a bit," she admitted.

"No problem." He jotted another note on the pad before him. "Not many classroom-educated people would. What I was saying..." He let the pen drop and looked up at her again. That was the first time she noticed how incredibly long and dark his lashes were, a silky frame for eyes that were too blue to belong to a man she had already decided to dislike. There was nothing in those eyes now but the professional interest of a teacher in a student. "...is that you are far too advanced for this class. You would be wasting your time here, and mine."

Why wasn't that the best news she had heard all day? She should be glad to get out of this class, this course, away from him...

She heard herself arguing, "I don't think so. I told you I can speak a little and I can understand a little more, but I can't read or write..."

His nod was dismissing a problem he had already considered and solved. "I'm going to put you in a more advanced class, and I'll tutor you in reading and writing. With the grasp of the language you already have, it shouldn't take you more than a couple of weeks to get the basics."

For just a second Callie was nonplussed, then her mind started racing. She tried to ignore the little jump of excitement that quivered through her pulses. Tutor? Had he said tutor? Hours in private sessions with this man—his apartment or hers? A whole series of crazy images flashed through her head and she knew instinctively that such an undertaking could be disastrous...never mind the fact that, for just a moment there, it had also been highly appealing. She grasped desperately for fleeting arguments against the suggestion. It was terribly unorthodox, it was entirely unexpected, it was simply ridiculous, it wouldn't work... And in the end Callie could only shake her head and say, "I need the course credit."

His eyes were bland and businesslike. If he had sensed any of her real reason for objection, he gave no sign of it. "What if I could get you earned credit for this course at the same time you're taking another? That would cut your time of course completion in half."

Callie had to think about that for a minute. Half the time meant half the money, and that was not an offer she could refuse lightly. But... "I—I don't think so," she stammered. "I'm really not that good, and I have other courses that will take a lot of my time...I really don't think I could handle private lessons on top of everything else..." In fact she was almost sure of it.

"You couldn't, huh?" He leaned back in his chair, one arm crossed over his chest to support the weight of his elbow, the finger he rested alongside his nose partially disguising from her the amused quirk of his mouth. His eyes glinted wickedly. "Come now, Miss Lester," he persuaded with an exaggerated show of patience. "If you're afraid that the—er—forced intimacy of private lessons might result in some indiscretion on my part, please put your mind at ease. I am always a perfect gentleman where my students are concerned, mostly because the erratic caprices of oversexed teenagers hold very little appeal for me." And he lifted one eyebrow infuriatingly. "Of course only you can judge how well you'll be able to keep your own urges under control, and if that is going to be a problem..." He trailed off with a negligent shrug, which only added insult to the implication.

At that moment Callie's greatest urge was to throw something at him. *Oversexed teenager...* controlling *her* urges... Her eyes narrowed to flickering charcoal slits, her knuckles whitened on the books that she still clutched protectively to her chest, and the muscles in her cheek tightened to outline a perfect triangle from temple to jaw. He watched the transformation with lazily disguised fascination, unaware, of course, that he was one of the few people ever privileged to see Callie Lester in a temper. But he would not have the satisfaction of seeing that temper explode, nor would she ever willingly accede to him the upper hand.

She forcefully relaxed her jaw muscles and the fists that were longing to fling her books in his face as she tilted her chin imperceptibly. "I hardly think that will be a problem," she returned coolly, "as I find the appeal of oversexed, egotistical university playboys incredibly easy to resist myself."

Was that a flicker of admiration in his eyes behind the winsome smile? Or maybe it was just male defense against an ego well-pricked, for he glanced down immediately and made another scrawling note on his desk pad. "Fine," he said easily. "Why don't you meet me in the registrar's office tomorrow afternoon at four, and we'll see if we can't get this thing straightened out?"

That appeared to be that. Callie could hardly
back out now without admitting that his assump-
tions about her reasons for reluctance were cor-
rect...which, of course, they were. She was aware
of having been bested by a master and did not like
the feeling at all, but above all else she would not let
him know it. She turned to go.

"By the way..."

Callie had to look back at him. His smile was
easy and relaxed as he stretched out in the chair
again, almost as though in a sign of truce. There
was none of the teacher-student posturing now,
none of the subtle sexual challenges, just a friendly
expression and a casual atmosphere. The battle, as
far as he was concerned, was behind them. "You
missed some pretty important information at the
beginning of the class," he said. "You might want
to catch up."

Callie regarded him warily. This sudden change
of attitude made her very uneasy. "Like what?"

He smiled. "Like my name. It's Sage McCormick."

Sage. She liked that. But she frowned, almost in
self-defense, and she challenged, "As in the brush
or the herb?"

His eyes sparked briefly. "Maybe both. Maybe as
in 'wise.' What about Callie? What's that short
for?"

Oh, he could be charming when he wanted to.
She would have to be very, very careful of that. She
twisted her own features into a semblance of a
haughty smile and gave a little toss of her head.

"That," she replied pleasantly, "is not relevant either."

He laughed softly, and his eyes moved over her briefly in undisguised appreciation of the entire package before coming to rest again with a twinkle on her face. "A woman with secrets," he observed. "I like that. Careful, though, I'm known for my deductive powers. I'll unravel all your secrets before I'm done."

Not, thought Callie as she turned to make as dignified an exit as possible under the watchful gaze of those laughing eyes, *if I can help it. No sir, not at all. . .*

Then she stopped and turned back once again. She had to know.

"At the beginning of class," she asked cautiously, hating to even bring the subject up but knowing it would nag at her constantly until she got an answer, "the second time you spoke to me in Russian, when you were laughing so hard—what did you say?"

His eyes twinkling merrily, once again he leaned back in his chair and rested his forefinger against the side of his temple, letting her read whatever she liked from that expression. And she read a great deal. "That," he replied simply, "will be *my* secret."

Callie was more convinced than ever that this whole thing had been a big mistake.

Chapter Three

It was eleven thirty in the morning and Callie felt as though she had already put in a full day of hard labor. All she wanted to do was go back to her apartment with its cool and impersonal beige and brown furnishings and lie down. Hopefully to forget the entire morning. But she had one stop to make first.

The student center was located in the center of the campus, and this close to lunchtime it was crowded. Callie caught a glimpse of her reflection in the glass door as she pulled it open and she winced. She looked like a refugee from the forties with her wilting hair and low-heeled shoes. The suit did absolutely nothing for her figure, which was, of course, why she had bought it in the first place—she had learned very early in her career that her job as translator was much easier if she faded into the background. Fortunately she still had enough tan left over from Argentina to get away without wearing stockings, but her makeup could definitely use some repair. All the laughter and young faces around her made her feel positively ancient.

Private lessons. Her inward groan almost became an audible one as she wondered how she had let herself be backed into such a corner. Well, it *was* the sensible thing to do, wasn't it? she tried to rationalize. She was here to complete a definite course of study in as short a time as possible and couldn't afford to let herself be distracted by sexy grins or taut muscles or wicked blue eyes. He had just been playing on her vulnerability today anyway. He had sensed she was nervous over a bad start and he was taking advantage of it. The possibility was perfectly plausible that he had had his fun now and would settle down and do his job... He was awfully good in Russian and, she had to admit grudgingly, he was probably one of the best teachers she had ever encountered. And hadn't he made it perfectly clear he wasn't interested in oversexed teenagers?

That even made her smile as she edged her way to the bulletin board. Callie could not remember ever having been a teenager, and as for oversexed...

Maybe that was one of the main motivations behind this entire project: a chance to live out the youth she had never had. Callie had worked since she was sixteen, and from the time she was six she had fallen naturally into a role reversal in which she was the mother and her mother was the child. There was no other alternative. Callie's mother, a generous, affectionate, but totally irresponsible woman, was one of those rare people who blissfully refused to adjust to the real world. She wandered through life with an ethereal smile and dreams of better days and was totally incapable of taking care

of herself, much less a daughter. The joys and trib-
ulations of growing up had passed Callie by, but an
early adulthood had given her advantages few people had. Callie had learned determination, courage,
and survival skills at an early age, and those skills
had carried her through high school with a full
scholarship to the local university, through four
years of study and part-time jobs, to a full-time job
and a part-time master's degree, and at last to the
career of her dreams. She should have been proud
of herself and what she had accomplished, but
through it all there had been something missing...the very same thing that now brought her to
the student center of a university campus with a
note card in her hand that said "Roommate
Wanted."

Callie had debated a long time about that. It was
not that she was unused to roommates: she had had
a succession of them, all of them only too happy to
share the rent with a person who was rarely ever
home more than two months out of the year. What
Callie was uncertain about was how she would like
living with a girl so much younger than she that they
could not possibly have anything in common, a student who might expect pajama parties and a series
of overnight dates and who knew what else. But a
two-bedroom apartment had been all Callie could
find, and absorbing the entire financial burden
herself would be impractical. She was just going to
have to learn to make adjustments to this new
lifestyle.

Callie was just affixing the thumbtack to the notecard when a small, white hand deftly removed it from her fingers. Callie turned, startled, to meet a petite, fuzzy-haired blonde in a calico prairie skirt and red T-shirt. The girl studied Callie's notice in myopic absorption through enormous, heavy-lensed glasses, and she read out loud, "Female wanted to share furnished two-bedroom apartment with same. Two blocks from campus. One fifty a month."

The girl looked up with an ingenuous grin, stuck out her hand, and announced, "Hello, roomie. I'm Tandy Stevens, and I can move in this afternoon."

Callie could not help responding to the grin, the impish little face, the outrageous assumption of the very young. But her smile was a little condescending. "Hello," she said. "My name is Callie Lester and that's my ad you're tearing in half."

Tandy paused with the two pieces of the notecard in her hand. Her muted green eyes, already magnified to three times their size by the glasses, widened so that they seemed to swallow up her whole face. "Well, what do you need it for? I'm here already." Then perception seemed to dawn slowly and she said, "Oh! You're worried I can't pay the rent. Hey, no problem," she dismissed it lightly. Her grin was positively infectious. "My dad's rich. Besides, my horoscope said. . . ." She turned to fumble in the oversized leather sack purse that was slung over her shoulder, producing at last a small scrap of newsprint. "Here it is! 'Domestic harmony is high-lighted today. New friends come your way.'"

She offered the paper for Callie's inspection, who said, her lips twitching with amusement, "You carry your horoscope around with you all day?"

"Well, sure." Tandy seemed amazed by the question. "It helps me keep in tune with the universal rhythms, you know. Hey, what sign are you?"

Callie was having a hard time keeping her laughter under control. The girl was an adorable child, but really... "Tandy," she began, "I don't think—"

"Doesn't matter," Tandy shrugged cheerfully. "I'm a Libra, so I can get along with anybody. So I'll just pack up my duffle bags and head over to the new place. Dorms are such a bore, aren't they?" She turned to go and just as Callie lifted a hand to stop her, Tandy suddenly remembered something. "Say," she inquired curiously, "what's the address anyway?"

Callie's attitude at that moment was, why fight Fate? She could do worse, she supposed, than a scatter-brained Libra with a rich dad and a pixie charm, and she had really been through so much today she simply didn't have the energy to argue. Maybe she should take a leaf from Tandy's book and check her horoscope: This seemed to be Callie's day for being backed into situations against her better judgment.

She decided to relax and enjoy it. "Don't you want to see the place first?" she offered with barely concealed amusement.

"No need. I trust you." And then those enormous eyes widened again. "Hey, I just remembered! I have a yoga class this afternoon. What time is it anyway?"

Callie glanced at her watch. "A little before noon." And then she looked at the epitome of impulse and disorganization before her and asked, "Don't you wear a watch?"

"Never," responded Tandy cheerfully. "How about I bring my stuff over this evening? You got anything in the fridge?"

"Not much," admitted Callie. "How do you get to class on time?"

"You've got to keep in touch with the universal rhythms!" responded Tandy with a grin, and then her eyes narrowed on Callie as though seeing her for the first time. She swept her up and down with the air of an expert jeweler scrutinizing a suspicious gem and made her judgment with a slight shake of her head. "If we're going to be roommates, hon," she pronounced, "we've got to get you some clothes." And then, as quick as a flash, the effervescent grin was back and she turned with a single birdlike movement to make her way to the door. *"Ciao!"*

Callie recovered herself just in time to call the address after her, and Tandy lifted her hand in acknowledgment. Callie did not have the slightest hope that her new roommate would ever find the apartment.

After that episode Callie knew that she had to sit down with a cup of coffee before even beginning the trek across campus to the sanctuary of her own apartment—a sanctuary that was soon to be invaded by an elfish force that Callie was sure, at the very least, would leave her life in even more of an uproar than it was now. And all that was assuming, of course, that young Tandy Stevens remained in touch with her universal rhythms.

Callie made her way slowly through the long line in front of the coffee machine, absently scanning the crowd. The noise in the high-ceilinged room was vivacious, energetic, and somewhat overwhelming to someone who was as mentally and emotionally exhausted as Callie. You're too old for this, she told herself wearily, and then found herself wondering if professors—in particular those wearing leather jackets and motorcycle boots—ever frequented the student center.

But a moment later she had cause to curse her wandering thoughts and the foolish reason for them. She turned, balancing her cup of coffee in one hand and her books in the other, took one step forward, and bumped into someone. Her books went flying, the hot coffee splashed partially on her hand and partially on the front of the man's wrinkled corduroy jacket, with the remainder forming a puddle around his shoes. She heard his small sound of dismay against her own gasp of chagrin, and she immediately joined in his efforts to brush the coffee stains off the light-colored jacket.

She expected abuse and profanity; what she got was a gentle, "Never mind, my dear, no harm done..."

Callie looked up in surprise into a pair of vague gray eyes, a kind face creased with lines of age and smiles and surrounded by shaggy silver hair. A professor, not a student. The way her luck was running today, she should have known. "But—but your coat," she stammered. "I'm terribly sorry—I'll pay the cleaning bill, of course. . ."

He laughed softly, and already his attention was wandering away from her. She got the impression that this man was incapable of concentrating on such mundane matters as coats and cleaning bills for more than a few seconds at a time. "This old thing? It's seen worse than coffee, I assure you. . ."

"This doesn't," said a voice from somewhere in the vicinity of her ankles, "appear to be your day."

Brad was on the floor, gathering up her books again. She had never been so glad to see anyone in her entire life. "Oh, Brad, thank you. I—"

She turned as Brad handed her books to her to make another apology, but the professor was already wandering away. "Ice for the hand," the older man commented absently, and Callie, vaguely under the impression that he was speaking in some sort of code, did not know what to say. He had disappeared into the crowd before she even got a chance.

She turned back to Brad with a dry grimace. "Great going," she groaned softly. "I've antagonized two professors and spilled coffee on a third and I've only been to one class. You're right. . .this is not my day."

Brad laughed. "Don't worry about old Chalmers. His head is so messed up from sniffing all that dope he whips up in his laboratory, he probably didn't even notice. He sure won't remember you ten minutes from now.''

Callie frowned a little, looking up at him. "Drugs?"

Brad shrugged. "Some kind of chemicals. He doesn't even teach here, just hangs around to give the place prestige. He's working on the cure for the common cold or something. Say. . ." His brow creased with concern as he took her fingers lightly between his. "You did get a burn, didn't you? Come on, I'll get you some ice."

"*That's* what he meant!" Callie exclaimed in dawning acknowledgment, as Brad was leading her across the crowded floor toward the ice machine. "It's really not necessary," she protested. "It's not that bad. . ." But as she had already recognized, today was not her day for making protests register or opinions firm.

"Here." Brad took her books from her and handed her a Styrofoam cup of ice. Callie resignedly scooped up a few crystals and began rubbing them over her slightly scalded hand.

"I looked for you after class," Brad commented, lounging against the ice machine. "Did you get it all straightened out with the Russian prof?"

Callie did not want to think about that. Instead she inquired curiously, "How did you do that? Find out which class I was supposed to be in?"

He grinned sheepishly. "I copied the program from the main computer bank, just to fool around with. I had no idea it would come in handy so soon.''

"You must know a lot about computers," Callie observed, wiping her damp fingers on her skirt.

He shrugged. "A little. I've been fooling with them for a few years." And his eyes lightened. This was obviously his favorite subject. "I've got a great system—took me two years to put together, but there's nothing that baby can't do. Some of the programs are out of this world. You'll have to see it sometime."

Callie laughed. She liked Brad; he reminded her of the brother she had always wished she had. "I wouldn't be able to tell one end of it from the other. I'll have to take your word that it's great." Then she inquired curiously, "So why are you taking BASIC Programming when you already know how to do it?"

An uncomfortable expression crossed Brad's face that made him suddenly look very young. Again he shrugged. "I guess I've been fooling around on my folks' money too long. They laid down the law— either get serious about school or get out. So I decided to go for Computer Science. . . ." He grinned, unexpectedly and endearingly. "Because it was the one thing I knew I wouldn't have to work hard at to pass."

Callie laughed. "I wish I had been that smart." She walked over to the trashcan to deposit the cup of ice, and he strolled with her.

"Russian, huh? How did you ever get interested in a thing like that?"

"It's my job," she replied brightly, and her smile softened as she turned back to him. Brad could be a good friend, and she did not want to leave room for any misunderstanding. "I'm not really a student," she confessed, "I'm an interpreter—that's what I do for a living. I'm just going back to school to brush up on a few more languages." And she laughed. "I'm really an old lady in disguise!"

Brad looked only impressed. "Far out," he murmured. "Who do you interpret for?"

Callie took her books and they started walking out. "Anybody who needs it. Businessmen mostly." And as they walked across the sun-strewn campus, she told him about her job and her travels; he listened in fascination and asked appropriate, incisive questions, and by the time they parted company at the corner of Callie's street and University Avenue, they were easy friends. Callie could use a friend right about then, and she was grateful.

She had only one class on Thursdays...Russian. Tomorrow her class schedule would begin in earnest, but today there was nothing for her to do but recuperate from the morning and try to prepare herself for the chaos her life was about to become. And she needed all the time she could get for that task.

Callie's apartment was like every other she had had in her life—bland, impersonal, hotel-room neat. There was nothing within it to even indicate human occupancy, and Callie barely gave it a glance as she dumped her books on the table and made her way to the bedroom, kicking off her shoes and stripping off her jacket as she went.

With a sigh she lay down on the hard, metal-framed bed with its beige ribbed spread, her hand resting over her forehead, her bare ankles crossed. Was it really possible that in a few hours she would be sharing this quiet domicile with a blond-haired whirlwind who carried her horoscope around like a talisman to ward off evil and studied yoga? No, decided Callie, that was entirely too much for her tired mind to accept. She must have imagined the entire episode.

She knew she should call Jerry. After all, he had done so much for her, it would only be polite, wouldn't it, to give him a call? She at least owed him the opportunity to say I Told You So.

Callie turned her head toward the phone on the wobbly bedside table, but made no move to reach for it. What did one say to a man who had been an on-and-off lover, part-time nemesis and full-time friend for over eight years? Wish you were here? Because Callie didn't.

Jerry Sloane was an investigative reporter for a Chicago newspaper. They had met quite by accident—he was the nephew of her first employer—but Callie thought they would have probably gone on to develop a relationship even if she had not decided to use his talents to further her own cause. He was easygoing, fun to be with, and relatively undemanding. His dedication to his own work made an understanding of Callie's involvement in her career a foregone conclusion, and as a natural side benefit, it precluded any thoughts of a committed relationship. When Callie flew off to London or Amsterdam or Rome, he was with another woman; when he was on the trail of a hot story, he did not ask if she had been with another man. When their paths crossed, they enjoyed their time together; when they were on opposite sides of the world, they rarely thought about each other, but a long-distance telephone call could pick up the threads of the relationship as though they had never been severed. It was easy, secure, and undemanding...and very empty.

Sometimes Callie worried about that. Why did Jerry's main appeal to her lie in the fact that he was incapable of, and uninterested in, making a full-time event of their relationship? Callie was honest enough with herself and aware enough of herself to know that she did not want to live the rest of her life in emotional sterility. A home, a family...those things she had never had and always wanted, those were the very things Jerry made it perfectly clear he had no intention of offering her. Yet she never looked any further than him.

And it was in the nature of their relationship that she could talk to him about it, and he would understand...albeit with a touch of humor.

"You have a Questing Beast to track down, Callie," he had told her with a soft laugh and a shake of his head. "You don't have time for home and hearth and tending the cradle. Never have and never will. You don't even want it, not really."

Callie's brows knit in puzzled curiosity. "Questing Beast?"

He nodded soberly. "The old-time knights in

search of the Holy Grail or the Dragon of Penzance or whatever the hell happened to be the latest fad...they didn't care what they were chasing and half the time didn't know. It was just an excuse for being on the road. A Questing Beast.''

Callie thought about that. A lot.

And she wondered what Jerry would say if she told him she was already having second thoughts about the way the latest tangent in pursuit of her mythological beast had taken her. They could laugh together about her first day of university life and it might make her feel better. But in the end he would have no advice to offer her, no judgments to make, no perceptive truths to point out. He knew as well as she did that this time she was in too deep— financially and emotionally—to back out. And he also knew that once she had decided on a course of action, sheer stubbornness would compel her to see it through. Perhaps one of Jerry's main disadvantages was that he knew Callie entirely too well.

He was the only person Callie had ever told about Jed Frye.

To this day Callie wondered if her life might not have been easier had she kept the secret to herself. Without Jerry's access to information, without his tenacious investigative techniques, without, in fact, his own personal interest to drive him, there would have been no hope or cause for hope. She could have kept her secret and kept her fantasies, dusty memories locked away in the attic of a child's imagination where they belonged.

But it was a matter of timing as much as anything

else. Jerry had come into her life when the trauma was still too fresh, the secret too burning, the compulsion too great to be put aside. He was a reporter. He knew people, he knew techniques. He could unearth the secrets buried within a newspaper morgue or the bowels of a moldy police station's records room with as little effort as it took Callie to think about it. Information poured into him constantly; he missed nothing. Callie could not turn down an opportunity so golden, and so she took that first and fatal step on a journey that had no end, never realizing that she was about to become addicted to something as pointless as a jigsaw puzzle with half the pieces missing.

They had known each other three weeks—long enough for Callie to trust him, long enough for him to accept her reasons for using him. They might, had things gone differently, even have fallen in love at that point. But Callie would not give it a chance.

Jerry studied the worn and wrinkled newspaper clipping she had given him without much show of surprise. "Sure," he said, "I've heard of Jed Frye. Who hasn't?" He returned the clipping to her with little more than a cursory glance. "Why?"

Callie said, speaking very carefully to restrain the trembling of her lips, "I want to find him."

Jerry laughed shortly, amusement and amazement mingling with the tolerant condescension in his eyes. He did not know Callie very well then— not well enough to know what a big mistake taking her lightly could be. "Nice trick if you can do it."

"I know I can't do it," she had returned evenly,

her face perfectly composed and expressionless. "Not alone. But you can."

That was when Jerry first began to suspect she was serious. He straightened up a little, his eyes growing cautiously alert. "What makes you think that?"

"Wouldn't you like to?" she pursued. Her face could become like stone when she wanted it to, shielding every emotion and hint of emotion from even the most probing observer. That was another thing Jerry had yet to learn about her.

"Sure," he admitted, still watching her carefully. "Me and every other reporter in the country, about fifteen thousand cops, and every G-man from the Secretary of State on down."

Callie simply nodded. "So," she said, "here's your chance."

Jerry had to laugh. It was more of a nervous reaction than anything else. "Right! I'll just run right out and do that. No problem." But Callie was not laughing, and his expression softened again into cautious curiosity. "Honey," he explained patiently, "a man doesn't get to be on the FBI's 'ten most wanted' list—and stay there for almost fifteen years—for nothing, you know. I mean, we're talking big-time bad guy here—"

"He was not a 'bad guy'!" Callie exploded passionately, startling him. "He never killed anyone!"

"Oh, yeah?" Taken aback by the glitter in her eyes and the fury in her voice, Jerry let his own tone rise in retaliation. "What about the four people in that car he blew up? What about the guard shot in that bank robbery and the five people killed in the riot? Coincidence, I suppose!''

"No one ever positively connected him with those things," Callie shot back. "There's no proof—"

"Whether he actually fired the gun or just gave the order is immaterial," Jerry returned shortly. "The man is a dangerous criminal." And then something in her face made him retreat a little and regroup. His tone became more rational. "Look," he explained, "at last count—besides the robberies and the *suspected*..." emphasizing the word with as little sarcasm as possible, he continued, "...murders, the charges against him include insurrection and conspiracy to overthrow the government. You can hardly get more criminal than that."

"Bureaucratic garbage," Callie retorted sharply. She felt compelled to defend herself, and quickly. "If he had lived in 1776 instead of 1966, he would have been called a patriot. All he was doing was looking for a better way—and he wasn't the only one. It was a whole movement; there were dozens of men like him—"

"Every one of whom," pointed out Jerry, "ended up either dead, in prison, or underground. Nobody even knows for sure which category this joker is in."

And then Jerry was surprised by what he thought was a glimmer of tears on Callie's quickly lowered lashes. He was more confused, more alert, and more cautious than ever. And now he knew without a doubt that she was very serious. He did not know quite how to handle this, nor what she expected of him, and he had to stop and think for a long time.

"Callie," he said at last, gently. He knew no way around the truth. "The man robbed banks. He used the proceeds from those robberies to finance terrorist activities. Innocent people got hurt. Maybe he was an idealist, but he was wrong. He was a criminal, Callie, not a saint. A highly educated, highly motivated, and very shrewd man—but a criminal nonetheless."

There was a long, long silence. And at last Callie said, so lowly he could hardly hear her, "I know."

She said nothing else. Jerry reached out and slowly took the news clipping from her, studying it. He would find nothing there he didn't already know. Callie knew he would not let it drop. Even if he had not cared for her, she knew he would not let it drop. "The man has been underground for five years," he said at last, still very carefully. "He has good cause to stay there. There's no statute of limitation on conspiracy and terrorism. Even if you could find him... Why would you want to?"

Callie slowly and carefully retrieved the clipping from him. Then she looked at him. "Because," she said quietly, "he's my father."

Callie sighed and turned her head toward the window, staring without seeing at the slanted rays of sun that spilled through the venetian blinds and made geometric patterns on the carpet. And so here she was, at the latest juncture in the never-ending road on which her quest had taken her, wondering how much longer it could possibly go on.

She was growing tired of the journey. She was

twenty-nine years old and what she had to show for her life was a map marked with meaningless parallel lines. She did not belong here, and she knew why. It had nothing to do with a university campus or an impossible course of study or even wasting time. It had to do with roads that led nowhere and chasing rainbows, and none of it was what she really wanted.

The trails she followed were long and convoluted with many twists and tangents along the way, but they were never circular. They never led home.

That was what left her feeling empty.

Chapter Four

Callie sank down into the stiff-backed chair outside the registrar's office and unobtrusively wiggled her aching feet out of her shoes, stifling a yawn. The small waiting room was crowded with students in worse schedule trouble than she, and Callie had had her eye on that chair for almost half an hour. It had been another long day.

The day had actually begun almost twenty-four hours before. Tandy had arrived shortly after five P.M., complete with eight crammed-full duffle bags and half a pickup truck full of other miscellanea. Callie now understood why dormitory life did not suit Tandy. The only interruption in the marathon of activity and chatter had been a short nap between four and seven A.M. It had resumed anew at seven with the vibrations of an operetta from the classical radio station shaking the walls and a profusion of rather nauseating odors emanating from the kitchen as Tandy prepared them both for early-morning classes.

Callie had forgotten what it was like to be nineteen years old and able to stay up all night talking about everything and nothing at all, but for the one night she had enjoyed the experience. She was paying for it today.

Tandy Stevens had burst onto the scene like a small tornado of sound and color—complete with an entourage of six hefty freshmen loaded down with bags and boxes—and Callie had no hope that her life would ever be the same again. Tandy was going to introduce her to the pleasures of yoga and TM, opera and television situation comedy. Tandy would do the cooking; Callie would do the housekeeping. Tandy would advise on everything from Callie's wardrobe to her love life and all Callie had to do was listen. Tandy was into science fiction, art deco, and open windows at night when the temperatures dropped below forty degrees Fahrenheit. She was not into silence, red meat, or studying.

Dinner was enthusiastically served at nine o'clock, accompanied by a stream of chatter and the light of two purple candles shaped like mushrooms. The indirect lighting, of course, was to forestall such pointless questions as "what is it?" and Callie thought it was probably just as well because she was sure she did not want to know. The exact nature of the dish was never revealed throughout a long discourse on its mind- and body-strengthening qualities, but Callie had a strong suspicion a primary ingredient was seaweed. That was when Callie realized that she should have fought harder for kitchen privileges.

Tandy never threw anything away. The entire

contents of her nineteen years of life were stuffed
into duffle bags and stacked in boxes against the
walls of Callie's apartment. Since every item they
unpacked had a story, not much progress was made
on that project during the night. Callie, who often
left the country for months at a time armed with no
more than one suitcase, was amazed at how one
small person could accumulate so much in so few
years. And she began to prepare herself for a domestic environment that was an absolute guarantee
of being anything but dull.

Callie smothered another yawn behind her hand
and blinked watery eyes, trying to stay awake. She
was glad she had not attempted to do this on her
own. She never would have gotten past the recep-
tionist's desk had she not been in the tow of a very
determined professor, and she felt sorry for the
students around her who had not had that advantage.

Today she had had her first classes in the Social
History of Developing Nations and Modern Economic Structures. Each class had sent her to the
library and kept her there for a total of four hours,
and all this was on top of a breakfast whose only
memorable quality was that it had been green. Tandy was also not into coffee and decried its addicting
and potentially hazardous qualities at every opportunity, but on that Callie remained firm. She
would not have survived the day without her
customary two cups in the morning. She was beginning to have doubts about surviving as it was.

She straightened up as she saw Sage come out,

and relief coursed through her when he cheerfully waved a new schedule and registration slip at her. She quickly slipped her feet back into her shoes and got up to join him. "Any problems?" she inquired.

"Hoards," he replied, but returned her papers to her with an air of victory. "Fortunately, there's nothing I like better than a challenge—unless its defeating an antiquated bureaucracy and cutting through miles of red tape with a single blow. You are now," he announced, savoring his triumph, "transferred from Russian I to Russian II, which meets on Wednesdays instead of Thursdays, with an open credit for Russian I at the end of this quarter, and as few other schedule changes as possible."

Callie laughed, relaxing for just a moment with gratitude. "It was nice of you to do this for me," she told him. "I would have made a mess of it myself."

He looked at her, and Callie was glad that the early awakening and her subsequent lack of interest in breakfast had left her time to pay a bit more attention to her personal appearance this morning. Tandy was right about one thing—her wardrobe did need a lot of updating, but the white skirt and pale-peach oxford shirt she wore were fashion basics that never went out of style. Callie had made a point to curl her hair and even guaranteed that it would hold by sweeping her hair back in perfect wings from the sides of her face with two gold barrettes borrowed from Tandy's collection. She had taken the time before meeting Sage to reapply her makeup—nothing elaborate, just a touch of peach lip color and soft green eyeshadow—and was confident that she looked a lot fresher than she felt. It had not occurred to her at the time to wonder why she needed to bolster her courage with makeup and curls for a meeting with Sage McCormick, but as he looked at her now she knew why. And she was glad she had done it.

"No problem," he said easily. "I got you into this, so it was only fair that I follow it through." And Callie thought she might have imagined that momentary spark of something other than impersonal interest that had been in his eyes. His arm brushed lightly against hers as he moved to point out something on her schedule form. "Actually, I think this will work out rather well for you," he said, and, with his eyes lowered, she could not see the hint of teasing that might have been there. "I've worked it so that you have Fridays free—good for all those romantic long weekends you'll undoubtedly want to take."

Callie shot him a quick glance but his face was perfectly bland. Nonetheless, she was aware of a slight quickening of her pulse. Irritated with herself, she tried to subdue it. Why did she let him do this to her when it was obvious he only wanted to annoy her? "Or maybe," she returned coolly, "we could use the time for my tutoring sessions."

He cocked his head in consideration. "Or maybe both," he agreed. There was no mistaking the twinkle in his eye this time, and it unsettled Callie more than she wanted to admit.

Today he wore a body-hugging cotton jersey with red-and-white striped sleeves tucked into the customary jeans, and he looked more like a student than a professor. Apparently there was no dress code for the university staff, but Callie was sure that if she had been in charge she would have enforced one. A man like Sage McCormick looked nothing but sexy in casual clothes, and he knew how to take advantage of it. He should have been perpetually confined to the rigors of a three-piece suit for the safety of all concerned. Callie wondered if he had much trouble with his female students...or if he would consider the kind of attention he undoubtedly attracted troublesome.

She managed to fix a disinterested little smile on her face, determined not to let him rattle her as he had done yesterday. "Let's try to keep this on a professional level, shall we, Professor?"

He immediately pulled a sober face that made Callie want to giggle—which, of course, was exactly what he had intended. "By all means," he replied mordantly and touched Callie's shoulder lightly to guide her through the crowd.

She was struggling to keep her tone businesslike. "We do need to discuss the lessons," she reminded him as they stepped out into the bright autumn sunshine. The reflected sunlight that glowed off the network of pristine white sidewalks wrapped warmth around a day that was cold on the inside, like reheated toast. Callie felt a chill on her shoulder when he removed his hand.

"My thoughts exactly," he agreed, and hooked

his fingers into his pockets as he strolled along beside her at an easy gait. His head was tilted back, shoulders relaxed, face catching the sun—a sensitive animal in tune with nature and reveling in it. Then he glanced at her, easily and unexpectedly. "What do you say to discussing it in..." He brought his arm up and looked at his watch. "About two hours, over pizza?"

Callie was completely nonplussed. She was not even aware that she had stopped walking until he lifted a quizzical eyebrow at her and inquired, "You did intend to eat tonight, didn't you?"

"Yes, but—"

"You've had a better offer?"

Callie thought about last night's seaweed casserole and could not prevent a rueful shake of her head. "No, but—"

"But what?" he challenged her directly. There was a hint of amusement in his aggressive stance as he stood before her, hands in pockets, feet planted firmly apart, blue eyes turning almost crystal in the sunlight. He enjoyed putting people on the defensive, that much was clear.

Callie did not know quite what to think. She certainly hadn't expected this. Why did she feel the need to be very, very cautious with this man? Her brows twisted into an unconscious frown of puzzlement and suspicion and she said the only thing she could think of. "Isn't it against the rules or something for professors to—be seen socially—with students?"

He chuckled. "Hardly. That would cut down on

a good three quarters of the campus scandals and then university life would be so boring the bottom would fall out of the enrollment quotients. But,'' he added, eyes still twinkling, ''if it bothers you, we'll make it as 'un-social' an occasion as possible. You'll just happen to wander into Jeno's about seven, I'll just happen to be sitting there alone, you'll just happen to stop by to say hello, and we'll just happen to share a pizza. Innocent enough?''

She fought hard with a tightening smile and lost. ''Sounds pretty cloak and dagger to me.''

He considered that thoughtfully for a moment and then grinned. The gesture was so boyish and endearing that it was completely irresistible. ''Yes, it does, doesn't it?'' he replied, pleased. ''Nice touch, I think.'' And he turned to go. ''Seven o'clock?''

''What about...'' She hesitated when he looked back at her and could have bitten her tongue, but it was too late to retreat now. ''What about,'' she continued stubbornly, ''what you said yesterday? About not being interested in your students.''

Of course the question implied that she had registered his innocent invitation to share a pizza as a display of ''interest'' in her, and Sage's face registered amusement with the fact and with her quick embarrassment. ''That,'' he pointed out with a wink, ''was before I found out you weren't an over-sexed teenager. I make no promises regarding mature and responsible twenty-nine-year-old women.'' And with nothing more than a grin and a ''See you tonight'' tossed over his shoulder, he disappeared into the entwining crowd.

Callie knew her face was softened with a reflective smile as she stood there looking after him, but she did not know why. She tried to shake herself out of it with a quick toss of her head as she turned in the direction of her apartment, but all the way home she felt like she was walking on air.

Tandy, whose own life was so full one would not think she had any time left over for vicarious thrills, threw herself into the project of preparing Callie for her "date" with all the enthusiasm of a mother sending her only daughter off to the senior prom. A skirt and blouse definitely would not do for the occasion. Neither would a simple pair of jeans and a jacket. Every article of clothing Callie owned, as well as Tandy's own considerable wardrobe, was strewn over the two bedrooms and spilled into the living room, a festival of color and disorder that filled Callie's previously bland apartment with a mad dormitory atmosphere that she found strangely exhilarating. Callie thought she was going to like having a roommate.

Of course, Tandy knew Sage McCormick and thought he was adorable. She enthused over how lucky Callie was, and how smart, to have snared him so quickly and refused to refer to the evening as anything other than a date no matter how hard Callie insisted that it was nothing more than a meeting to discuss her lessons. It wasn't long before Tandy had Callie thinking in terms of a romantic encounter, and that, of course, only made Callie nervous.

At last dressed in jeans, bulky-knit leg warmers,

and an oversized sweater with raglan sleeves pushed up to exactly three quarters of an inch below the elbow—no more, no less—and belted around her hips, Callie set off. The small leather purse with its long strap worn in a diagonal fashion across her shoulder was Callie's; everything else, including pointed-toe boots that were a little tight, had been garnered from Tandy's closet. Callie was both amused and pleased. She never would have taken her roommate for a fashion expert at first glance, but she certainly did seem to have a sense for the latest trends. Shopping was one of Callie's first priorities.

Jeno's was the student gathering place and, as such, reflected all the atmosphere of a university campus. It was brightly lit, crowded, and cheerful with the noise of fifty students unwinding from the rigors of the day. The brick walls were covered with colorful glass-framed posters, and a continuous loop tape of popular music played in the background. Lacquered pine tables and benches were set in pits and alcoves at various elevations, giving the impression of space to a place that was really very small. For a moment Callie stood there absorbing the bustle and the laughter, the aroma of tomato sauce and garlic, and letting it take her back ten years. Then she saw Sage stand and lift his hand to her.

He had secured one of the few private tables in the place, and at first Callie was glad. The round table was set in a small circular niche one step above the main floor, with two ladder-back chairs instead of benches. It offered them privacy, to be sure, but Callie thought that very fact would draw more attention to them than if they had sat out in the open with the rest of the students.

What difference does it make? she scolded herself irritably as she made her way over to him. You're making entirely too big a deal out of this thing. . .

"Perfect timing," he greeted her, pulling out her chair. "We should make a regular thing of this secret tryst business."

Callie saw the twinkle in his eye as she was seated and opened her mouth to protest, but he forestalled her.

"I've checked my schedule," he said, suddenly serious as he returned to his own seat, "and I'm afraid we can't make your lessons on Fridays. How about Tuesdays and Thursdays instead? From three to five."

Callie hesitated. Four hours a week? That was heavier than any other class she was taking. That sinking feeling overwhelmed her again, and she wondered how she would ever make it. But the last thing she wanted to do was let him know she might not be able to handle it, so she only sipped casually from her water glass and inquired, "Why not Fridays?"

The spark was back in his eyes again. "Long romantic weekends, remember? I've got a social life to consider, too, you know."

Callie tried not to smile at him. "Tuesdays and Thursdays will be fine," she told him primly.

"Good," he said easily. "Now that business is

out of the way, we can get down to the serious stuff.''

Callie lifted an inquiring brow. "Like what?"

He leaned back in the chair, relaxing so easily that Callie could not help doing the same. "Like," he suggested, "arranging one of those long romantic weekends...together."

Callie could not help laughing. How dare he be so charming? Someone should make a law. "Sorry," she responded, the subtle spark in her own eyes masked by the severe tone, "I'm not that kind of woman."

Sage smiled at her, a kind, intimate smile that somehow disturbed Callie more than his outrageous flirtation had done. "You have a nice laugh," he said softly. His eyes moved over her face in gentle assessment and approval. "I thought you would." The fabric of his gray tweed sweater tightened across the muscles of his upper arm as he reached for his own water glass, but not drinking from it, just lightly holding it with his fingers curled around the base. His attitude was casual and friendly, and the easy warmth in his eyes was contagious.

"You're letting the first-week rush get to you," Sage observed mildly. "Not a good idea. Try to relax and go with it; you're so uptight now you'll talk yourself into a breakdown by midquarter if you don't stop taking school so seriously."

Callie arched her brows, both surprised and a little touched by his concern. If he displayed this kind of personal care to all of his students, he must be a very good teacher indeed. "It's not serious?" she challenged.

Again a smile deepened one corner of his lips and made him look at the same time both sweet and mocking. "Not so much you can't laugh about it. You need to laugh more."

The waitress arrived then, breaking the mood of intimacy that he had generated so easily and unexpectedly. After a momentary consultation they ordered a pepperoni pizza and a pitcher of sangría, and Sage turned back to her.

"So," he invited expansively, "Callie Lester, age twenty-nine, single, formerly of the University of California, Berkeley, University of South Carolina, and Trans World Business Systems, to name a few—tell me about yourself."

Callie sat back, duly impressed, and her eyes widened in a mixture of amazement and self-defense. "Why don't you tell *me*?" she suggested. "Sounds like you know more than I do already." Then her brows came together in a faint semblance of a puzzled frown. "How do you know all that anyway?"

He shrugged. "The Computer Age is a marvelous thing. All I had to do was key in a request for a schedule change on your number and all of this fascinating information came spilling out. It was completely out of my control, I assure you."

"May be," Callie responded with a philosophical shrug of her own, "but the Computer Age has just swallowed up half our dinner conversation. No point in being redundant."

He chuckled. His eyes crinkled nicely when he did that. "Not necessarily," Sage pointed out.

"There's still a lot left to be discovered. Start with your life story; I'll tell you when I get bored."

Callie looked at him for a moment, then laughed helplessly. He was totally irrepressible and there was no point fighting it. "All right," she conceded. "Prepare to be bored." The waitress set the sangría on the table and Callie settled back as Sage poured two glasses. "Between the lines—and also between Berkeley and USC—I worked at all kinds of odd jobs, from legal secretary to French tutor..."

"You weren't born?" Sage interrupted, passing her glass to her.

"Oh, I see." She nodded soberly, her eyes twinkling as she fell into the spirit of the game. "Callie Lester came into the world one dreary winter day twenty-nine years ago in the little town of Modesto, California," she began dramatically, widening her eyes for effect. "The winds howled and a raging snowstorm pelted the windows..."

Sage's eyes sparked. "Winds rarely howl in Modesto," he pointed out. "And as for snowstorms..."

"Metaphorical winds," she assured him, pretending annoyance. "May I continue?"

He inclined his head graciously and made a benevolent gesture with his hand, his eyes dancing. Callie was enjoying this, more than she had ever thought possible. How long had it been since she had relaxed enough to enjoy anything? It was like being young again.

"At any rate," Callie continued determinedly,

"with appropriate theatrics and fanfare, I made my grand entrance on the scene. . ."

"Born to?"

She scowled at him. "Shall I tell this, or will you?"

He quirked an eyebrow in mock chagrin. Perhaps the best part was that he was enjoying her company as much as she was his. She could see it in his face, in his eyes, in every easy movement. "Many pardons," he said. "Please go on."

Callie took a sip of the fruity drink and looked at him. "Born to," she said deliberately, "one Isadora Lester. . ."

"Isadora." Sage smiled reflectively, but Callie should have been warned by the mischievous spark in his eyes. "I like that name. Who else but an Isadora would name her child California?"

The widening of Callie's eyes and her quick rush of color were not feigned. "Unfair!" she exclaimed. "You peeked!"

"I told you," he reminded her, "I'm an expert at uncovering secrets." Then he winked at her. The gesture was quick and intimate and it caused an unexpected little thrill to flutter in Callie's stomach. "Don't worry though," he assured her. "I'm also very good at keeping them."

Callie laughed to hide her sudden nervousness. "You'd really have to know my mother," she explained, "to appreciate the name. I mean, she was the original drifter." Callie's smile was affectionate. "Adorable, but a real space cadet."

Sage sipped his drink. "No father?"

It was an innocent comment, and one Callie should have expected. Quickly she lowered her eyes and turned her attention to her drink, but not before Sage saw the flash of truth there. And, of course, he picked up on it immediately.

"I'm sorry," he said gently. "It's none of my business."

Callie tried to smile, but she kept her eyes on the ice cubes she was busily pushing around with her straw. She gave a fair semblance of a negligent shrug. "I was a love child before such things were popular," she told him. "I never knew my father."

Sage nodded, his eyes quiet and kind, and when Callie glanced at him, she thought for a moment he really did understand. "Are you sensitive about it?" he inquired.

Now Callie could smile, though it was a little sad. "Not really," she admitted honestly. "I suppose it would have been a lot worse if I had had any other kind of mother, but to her it was the most natural thing in the world and I never felt the stigma growing up. Living with Isadora was like walking through the pages of a fairy tale, anyway, and she always turned to another story whenever she got to the part about the Big Bad Wolf."

Sage's expression was gently puzzled. "You mean she never told you about your father?"

This was getting difficult. Callie lowered her eyes and sipped the sweet red mixture through the straw, fighting what had suddenly become a powerful urge to tell him everything. It would have been so easy. He made it so easy. "Yes," she admitted carefully, "she told me about him. He was a med student when they met, they had a brief passionate love affair, he graduated and moved on. He never knew about me."

"What a strange feeling that must be," Sage reflected softly, "to know you have a father out there somewhere you've never met..."

He did understand. He understood and the simple, unpremeditated warmth of it reached out to her like an unexpected embrace. Callie felt something go soft in her and she confessed without meaning to, "I guess most of my life I've been looking into the eyes of strangers, wondering if each man on the street could be he..."

Sage nodded, instantly grasping both the circumstances and the emotions with an innate perception that could only be born of genuine caring. "And you wouldn't even recognize him if you met him," he observed in quiet wonder.

Callie thought of the blurry wire-service photo fifteen years old—a man with shoulder-length dark hair and an alpaca jacket, looking away from the camera and so far in the background that nothing about his features was distinguishable. And she thought back to Jerry's first incredulous observation after he had agreed to undertake the project, "You've never even seen him—you wouldn't recognize him if you found him!" But Callie knew she would. There would be something there, something that would reach out to her, something she would recognize calling her home...

"My mother," she said softly, looking into her

glass, "said he had sea-faring eyes. . ." And then she smiled a little, glancing up, trying to dismiss the reverie that had come upon her so quickly and so inadvisably. . .trying to dismiss the urge to tell him everything. It would have been so easy. "Her way of saying that he was a wanderer, I guess," she explained with more nonchalance than she felt. "One of those restless people always looking to the next horizon. . ."

"Like you," Sage observed gently, and for just a moment Callie was taken aback. The simple statement unexpectedly touched something so deeply buried within her that she had never before been aware of its existence. . . *Like you*. Like her father. She needed to be like someone, to know that there was continuity handed down, even if the legacy was nothing more concrete than a need to roam the earth in search of unknown treasures and nebulous challenges. What had her father been looking for? she wondered. And was he still searching?

The pizza arrived then, a welcome distraction from the sentimental, dangerously disturbing mood that had come upon her, and Callie greeted it enthusiastically. She had to remind herself that this was nothing more than a casual meeting with a man whose only purpose in her life was to instruct her in Russian, and if she were not careful, she would be spilling out her soul to him like a penitant in a confessional booth. Sage could make her feel so comfortable; he had put her so quickly at ease that she was acting like a lonely child aching to have someone to share her secrets with. Callie had to remember that he was a stranger, a passerby in her life, and there was danger in getting too close.

"Marvelous," she murmured as she bit into the thick-crusted pizza. "Hmm. I didn't realize how hungry I was."

Sage agreed. "If you want good pizza, the only place to go is near a university campus. Holds true all over the world." Then he inquired casually, "Do you know his name?"

Callie swallowed slowly. Why had she had that suspicion that he would not be waylaid so easily? And why did his interest, so genuine and unfeigned, pull at her with such gentle persuasion, enticing confidence she had no right to give?

She touched her napkin to her lips and took another long sip of the sangría. When she looked at him, her smile was easy, but her eyes firm with a message he could not mistake. "How long have you been at the university?" she inquired pleasantly.

The acknowledgment in his eyes was only half acceptance, the other half compromise. His smile assured her he would not push for too much too soon, his eyes told her he understood the pain. "Five years," he answered. "But we haven't finished with your life's story yet. Time enough later for mine." His eyes twinkled, letting her relax. "It's very short."

So Callie talked, drinking more than she ate, telling him the stories of her career and her travels, growing comfortable with the lively interest in his eyes, and warming to his quiet encouragement to reveal more and more about herself. It was clichéd but it was true: In a matter of a few hours, Sage had made her feel as though she had known him all her life, and the shields she usually built against strangers melted into nothing more than sheer curtains, allowing him easy access to whatever he pleased.

The crowd had thinned somewhat by the time she finally paused for breath, the atmosphere was more subdued, the background music had made the full circle to soft hits. A slice of pizza was cold and picked over on Callie's plate, and only orange and lemon slices remained in the bottom of the sangría pitcher. Little sleep and too much drink were sneaking up on Callie; she could feel it tingling in the tips of her fingers and surrounding her with a blanket of euphoric lethargy. She felt good, and she didn't even mind being so tired.

Sage smiled as she smothered a yawn with cupped hands, and he signaled for the check. "I'm sorry," she apologized. "I have this roommate who believes life doesn't start until after dark, and I'm a day person myself."

"So." Sage glanced at the check and reached for his wallet. "We're up to the present. How did you end up here registered in the wrong class with a night-owl roommate?"

How did you end up here. . . It was a good question. Would Sage be surprised if he knew the answer?

The details of that destiny-changing phone call came drifting back to Callie. Her heart had been in her throat, her hand wrapped tightly around the telephone cord that seemed to her at that moment to be a lifeline to hope, and she had inquired of Jerry as calmly as possible, "How can you be sure? How can you be sure Jed Frye is hiding out on a university campus in Michigan?"

And Jerry had returned, equally as calmly, "I just told you. I can't be sure—"

"You were sure enough to pay a hundred dollars for the information!" Callie's control had begun to slip, tension cracked in her voice. "You trusted your source enough to lay down your own money on him! For heaven's sake, Jerry, don't play games with me now—"

"Damn it, Callie, do you think I'm that stupid?" His own voice had snapped back at her with the stress she had communicated to him. "I didn't say I doubted my source. I don't hand out that kind of money to anybody who isn't straight with me, but he could be wrong."

"Tell me about him," Callie had insisted, her voice hard with restrained emotion. "Tell me about this famous source of yours."

Jerry had taken a deep, calming breath. "You know I can't do that," he said at last, quietly. "He's a guy, that's all, a part of the underground network, a leftover from the sixties. He helps me out with street work sometimes. He knows Frye— or he used to. He heard I was interested in the story, and all he said was that the latest had placed him at the university...and he didn't even know what he was supposed to be doing there. No clues as to his new identity or even if he had one, and I couldn't pin him down on a date...it could very well be that he surfaced there years ago and is long gone by now..."

"But," Callie had interrupted firmly, "you don't think so."

There followed a long silence. "No," he had admitted finally. "I don't think so." And there had been reluctance in his voice as he weighed his options. "Honey, there are things going on at that campus that—well, they smell of Frye's work."

"What kind of things?" she had demanded.

"No, I'm not getting into that without more proof; it'll only set you off half-cocked again. But, Callie, don't you see what a crazy long shot this is? You have nothing to go on..."

"I'll reimburse you the hundred dollars," Callie had said.

"I don't want reimbursement. It's my story, remember..."

She laughed as she looked at Sage now. It's a long story, she thought. A very long story...

"The roommate was more of a matter of being taken by storm than personal choice," she answered his questions in reverse order. "The registration was because I haven't yet learned to argue with a computer, and I'm here..." She tipped her glass up to extract the last droplets of wine from the melting ice cubes. "Because of one of the best language programs in the country."

He placed two bills on the table and inclined an inquiring eyebrow at her, asking if she were ready to leave. "But," he pointed out as Callie slid back her chair, "you're majoring in Mideastern Affairs, not languages."

She nodded. She felt the warm supportive touch of Sage's hand on her back and Callie almost forgot what she was going to say. Somewhere during the course of the evening this encounter had turned into all Tandy had predicted it would and everything Callie had so vehemently denied, and the realization set off a small flutter of excitement in her chest. Sage was no longer a stranger; it was no more a teacher-student relationship...at least not on Callie's part. She wondered what Sage was thinking, if he was really as interested in her as he pretended to be, or if he treated all his students this way. His female students, Callie mentally corrected herself, with the stern reminder not to take him too seriously. No man with his vibrant good looks and easy charm should be trusted for anything beyond a mild flirtation...but even the possibility of a flirtation held unprecedented appeal for Callie.

She glanced at him, and there was nothing more than alert curiosity in his eyes. She was reminded of his question. "I already have a degree in languages," she explained. "Even though I'm majoring in different languages this time, I needed a program that would reflect a broader field of study, and Mideastern Affairs is as close as I could get."

Was that sudden skepticism she saw in his eyes? Or perhaps a more intent interest than her simple explanation warranted? Callie could not be sure, and it confused her. For the moment he looked at her it almost seemed as though he were thinking of something else, seeing something he did not like, and that made Callie very uneasy. Then he smiled at her; she felt his arm slip around her waist. "Careful of the step," he advised, and lent her his support as she stepped down. The high heel of the unfamiliar boot caught on the edge of the step and she stumbled a little; she reached automatically for Sage's hand.

She felt the clasp of his hand and the hardening of the muscles of his arm as he righted her. It was a good feeling, causing another unexpected quickening of Callie's pulses. His eyes twinkled in mild amusement as he glanced down at her. "You're a little tipsy, aren't you?"

Callie knew she should have been embarrassed but she wasn't. "Too much stress and too little sleep," she admitted philosophically, "and I guess I forgot about the sledgehammer effect of sangría."

He cocked his head quizzically. "Sledgehammer?"

She nodded, carefully negotiating her way around the tables with his assistance. "It sneaks up on you when you're not looking and hits you like a sledgehammer," she explained. *Just like you do, Professor Sage McCormick. Just like you do . . .*

Callie glanced up at Sage as they stepped out of the restaurant. The night air bathed her face like a cool cloth, refreshing and rejuvenating. Her mind was clear, but the warm drowsiness of sangría and Sage's arm around her waist lingered in her body. She was relaxed and comfortable walking with him like this, as though it had always been this way. "And now we know all about me," she said.

"What about you? How did you come to be here?"

He breathed deeply of the crisp dark air, his exhalation left a faint ghost of frost against the night. His face was shadowed and gentled by the aura of the streetlight, and Callie wanted suddenly to reach up and touch it, to brush her fingers over his curls, to trace the shape of his eyes... "It's an easy job," he responded offhandedly. "Leaves me plenty of time for the more important things in life."

"Like what?"

The spark in his eyes was an answer that generated an immediate and leaping thrill of anticipation in her. "Like this," he said, and he turned, circling her with his arms, stepping close to her.

Callie felt a rush of awareness, a tingling in her cheeks and her fingertips, and a sudden jerking of her heart as he bent his face close to hers. His arms were a light embrace, his fingers strong against her back, his thighs brushing hers. And his eyes were as deep as the night sky and as filled with multitudinous, flickering lights.

Then there was a sound, echoing footsteps on the sidewalk behind them. Sage stiffened, immediately alert, and Callie's senses returned with a rush. She quickly stepped away as the figure approached, turning to hide her embarrassment. What did she think she was doing, anyway? Wasn't it she who only this afternoon was concerned about being seen socially with a member of the staff? And here she was about to be swept away by passion with him in the middle of a public campus, in plain view of anyone who wished to see...

You've got a crush on your teacher, she scolded herself miserably, *just like any other twelve-year-old in the country...*

Callie did not realize that in stepping back she had placed herself in the shadows of a long hedge that ran along the sidewalk dividing the campus from the public street, and the owner of the intruding footsteps had no way of knowing she was there. He saw Sage though and greeted him easily by his first name.

Callie did not imagine it; she was certain Sage was uncomfortable in the presence of this stranger. Was he embarrassed, too, by being caught in what could be considered a "compromising situation" with one of his students?

He stepped quickly in front of the boy with a dark curly hairdo and a droopy black mustache, and he spoke to him lowly and rapidly—in Russian. It was almost more as though Sage did not want Callie to see the boy than that he was embarrassed about being seen with her. She did not understand, and his entire attitude made her very uneasy. She could not understand what he was saying. Why then, did she feel almost certain that Sage was warning the boy of her presence? Why didn't he just bring her forward and introduce her?

The entire interchange lasted no more than thirty seconds, but it left a definite and disturbing impression on Callie. The young man with the black mustache glanced in her direction, seemed to discern her figure in the shadows, and proceeded to mumble something in English that was not meant for her

ears. He ended with a reminder about a Tuesday-
night meeting before he turned and walked abruptly
back the way he had come. Sage stared after him
for a moment, shoulders squared, hands thrust in
his pockets, and a strange glint in his eye that
looked totally out of character for him...or
perhaps Callie just imagined it.

He turned and strolled back over to her just as
though nothing at all were wrong, but his mood was
somehow subtly altered. He seemed stiffer, preoccupied, his thoughts no longer with her. "I'll walk
you home," he volunteered. "I assume it's within
walking distance?"

She nodded, watching him. The warm euphoria
of sangría and contentment was gone, and she felt
only cold and very alert. "Two blocks down," she
said. "But you don't have to..."

He took her arm firmly. His fingers were strong
and impersonal. "It's not a good idea for a woman
to walk alone at night through the campus." His
tone was grim. "There are too many unsavory types
hanging around."

Callie did not know how to argue with that. She
really didn't have the energy to try.

For a time there was nothing but the sound of
their footsteps on the damp, cold concrete, an occasional burst of laughter from a group of students returning late from the library or early from a party,
the slow passing of cars on the street next to them, a
brief and raucous blare of a radio, then more
silence. Callie tried to subdue the nervousness that
had come upon her with his sudden change of

mood. And she tried to ease him out of it. She glanced up at him. "How did you get interested in Russian?" she asked casually. "Where did you learn to speak it so well?"

He smiled at her, but it was a vague gesture, and his features were veiled. "Here and there," was all he would answer.

She was foolish enough to pursue it with a laugh that sounded hollow even to her own ears. "Now, that's hardly likely! Spanish, yes—French, maybe—but Russian is not something you just pick up on the streets."

They were in front of her apartment and she stopped. He looked down at her with a smile that was as distant as the fading moon, cold and unrevealing. "Maybe," he said smoothly, "I learned it from a friend. And maybe I'm really an international spy disguised as a mild-mannered professor. And maybe. . ." Sage brushed at her bangs with the tip of his finger, and for just a moment it seemed as though his expression softened. "A little secrecy is good for the soul."

Then he turned with no more than a reminder that she was to meet him in his office Tuesday afternoon for her first lesson, and he was gone.

Callie stood there looking after him for a moment, feeling suddenly cold, fighting off despondency, wondering what happened. She liked him. She liked him more than she should have, more than was wise... And she kept remembering that hard look on his face as he stared after the boy with the mustache, the aggressive stance of his body, the cold mood that had come over him afterwards. In retrospect, the entire scene looked sinister. There was no other word for it, and it made her shiver as she turned to go inside.

She wished he had kissed her.

Sage McCormick walked briskly with his hands in his pockets, his shoulders back, his head up. His catlike eyes missed no detail of the shadowy path before him, his flared nostrils and alert muscles drawing every nuance from the night air around him. When a shadow broke away from the darkened edges of the sidewalk and fell into step beside him, Sage did not break his pace.

"Cute trick," the man beside him commented.

Sage did not reply.

"Not too many with her talents around." The man spoke in a twangy midwestern drawl that was eminently suited to his greasy, shoulder-length hair, scruffy beard, and irritating habit of chewing on grass stems. He wore a floppy-rimmed sombrero-type hat with the crown cut out, dusty jeans, and knee-length fringed leather boots. His black T-shirt had an upside-down "Z" on the front and "Murder Babies" written in dripping red letters on the back. "I mean, right out of Argentina and all. Think she might be any help to us?"

Sage did not look up. His voice was curt. "She's straight. Leave her out of this."

The man beside him chuckled. It was a low, rolling, ugly sound. "Nobody's *straight*, man. Haven't you figured that out yet? At the very least . . ." And he shot Sage a glittering look filled with malevolence beneath slanted lashes. "Bet she could procure us a little Columbian gold. What do you think?"

Sage's muscles bunched ominously across his shoulder blades, and the shadows hid the tightening muscles of his face. His tone was conversational. "I think sometimes you believe your own propaganda, Axom."

Again the man chuckled. "And I think, much as I hate to admit it, you're not as dumb as you look. I was against bringing you in, you know..."

"That makes two of us," Sage muttered under his breath.

"But the boys," continued Axom easily, matching his long, loose-limbed stride to Sage's, "they had other ideas...and I guess we ain't been disappointed yet. You're pulling your weight. Like this broad, for instance..."

Sage stopped suddenly. His eyes met the smooth reptilian ones of the other man with a sharp glitter that would have frightened any other man. But George Axom and Sage McCormick were too much alike, too well-matched, and too equally experienced to ever pose a threat to one another. It was a standoff. Sage said very lowly, "Did it ever occur to you that the whole world doesn't revolve around this damn organization? Don't I get any personal life at all?"

Axom's smile was sweet and icy. "No," he said simply. "You know the rules as well as I do, man. Once you're in, you're in." He tossed the blade of grass he had been chewing onto the sidewalk and turned away. "Keep an eye on the broad," he added carelessly over his shoulder. "You never can tell when she might turn out to be useful."

For a moment Sage simply stared after him, fists clenching in his pockets, eyes narrowed and hard. Then he swung away in the opposite direction, back toward the place he had left his motorcycle. His shoulders were slightly hunched this time, his pace a bit slower, his expression thoughtful.

He wished he had kissed her.

Chapter Five

"Problems?"

Callie jumped a little at the sound of the voice, but it was only Brad. It seemed as though everywhere she turned lately he was there...and usually he appeared just when she needed a friend. She straightened up from the wall of the building against which she had been leaning, lost in thought, but the preoccupied scowl only lightened slightly as she looked at him. "You could say that," she muttered. "I've got a paper to write and the library doesn't have the research material I need... Or, rather, they do, but they're being used. And I don't know when I'm going to have time to come back."

"Hmmm." Brad pulled a contemplative face for just a minute, and then his irrepressible grin broke through. "Lucky for you, as always, I was here. Come on." He touched her shoulder lightly. "Allow me to once again solve all your problems and put your life in order."

Callie laughed and let him lead her down the steps. Whatever else Brad was, he was always a wel-

come change of pace in her day. It probably had
something to do with his youth.

"We can use my system to hook up to any information network in the country," he told her as they
walked across the lawns away from the building.
Again Brad flashed her that grin and said, "Why it
can even write your report for you if you want."

It took Callie a minute to understand what he was
talking about. "Oh, Brad, I don't know how to
work a computer!"

"Kid's stuff," he assured her. "Besides. . ." His
hand fell easily on her shoulder. "That's what I'm
here for."

Outside the dormitory Callie hesitated. "Am I allowed in here?"

Brad laughed and bounded up the steps.
"Where've you been? You never heard of coed?"

That did not precisely answer Callie's question,
but she followed him anyway. It would be rude to
turn away now, and Callie valued Brad's friendship
too much to risk it.

The small room was typical of any dwelling that
accommodated two men. The walls were covered
with posters and banners, the narrow beds piled
with books and laundry—some clean, some not—
and a bicycle leaned against the wall next to an en-
tertainment center that accommodated a stereo and
a portable television. The closet door was half open
and so were most of the dresser drawers; empty beer
cans were stacked on top of a small wood-tone
refrigerator. The place was not a pigsty, but it was
far from tidy; it simply exuded a cluttered at-

mosphere of two busy lives, just like any dorm room should. Just like any dorm room...except for one thing.

The desk before the window was very much like Callie's desk at home—with a goose-necked lamp, a stack of books, and a portable typewriter. Next to it were sheaves of paper stacked not very neatly. But the other desk, the one closest to Callie, seemed to take up half the room and would have been more appropriate for the war room of a national defense center than in a young man's bedroom. It was long and wide with a typing wing that protruded into the center of the floor. Attached shelves rose toward the ceiling, and those shelves were crammed with folders of floppy disks, computer paper, and several high-tech mechanical boxes whose functions Callie could not fathom. This desk, too, was scattered with beer and soft-drink cans, a half-eaten package of cookies, crumpled papers, and an empty can of peanuts, but between the mess a silent terminal screen glowed omnisciently, almost beckoningly.

Callie took in the setup appreciatively. "Your folks must be pretty rich," she commented, but Brad did not answer.

Brad followed the compelling beacon of the glowing screen unerringly, touched something on the desk and said, "Computer on."

From one of the boxes on a shelf, a mechanical voice responded, "Ready. Enter function."

Callie gasped, her eyes snapping around toward the source of the box and widening in amazement. "Just like *Star Trek*!" she exclaimed.

Brad grinned, obviously pleased with her reaction. "I'm just showing off," he admitted, as she approached the desk cautiously. "The things you can do with voice control are really very limited, and, of course, it's not the computer talking back— it's a recording that responds to the computer signals." But he could not resist showing off one more time. He sat down behind the desk, leaned back in his chair, and commanded, "Enter Network One."

There was a flickering on the screen and a row of numbers and letters rolled downward. The raspy voice box announced, "Function available. Please enter menu selection."

Callie was speechless, but Brad was already growing bored. He switched off the voice control and began tapping on the keyboard. "That was the university network," he explained. "You can't get anything out of that that you couldn't get in the library. What we need to do is plug into CompuServe."

She watched as he picked up the telephone receiver on the desk, dialed a number, and placed the receiver on yet another mechanical box attached to the computer. "We can go from here to any university in the world," he explained, "any library or research facility that participates...up to and including the Library of Congress. We'll get a complete listing of every article that's ever been written on your subject—even if it hasn't been published yet, the names of people doing research on your subject, even cross-references on current events relative to it. . . you name it, you got it. Have a seat.''

Callie sank rather numbly at the foot of the bed beside him and watched in growing respect and amazement as he put the world of information at her fingertips.

Brad explained each step to her as he went through them and, in his typically carefree and generous way made the computer available to her even when he was not present. Callie did not think she would ever go that far, but it was a power thrill to be able to follow his instructions and call up information from any source in the world. He showed her how to obtain a printout of the information she wanted and how to skip over that which she did not need. Soon Callie was confident enough to press the buttons that entered the command without Brad's standing over her shoulder. As she worked at the computer, he took two soft drinks from the refrigerator, handed her one and stretched out on the bed with the other one for himself.

''I can't believe it.'' Callie must have said that fifty times within an hour. She watched another page of computer notes roll out of the printer, shaking her head in wonder. ''I can write a report almost as fast as I can read one.'' She turned to Brad. ''Do you realize this would have taken me days—*days* to do the conventional way?''

He winked at her. ''The wonders of modern science.''

A niggling thought, barely formed, titillated Callie. Maybe it had something to do with the sudden opening of a door on a whole new and exciting world, maybe it was more the spirit of excitement and mischief generated by Brad's sheer youth. She remembered what Sage had said yesterday about punching a button on a computer and receiving her life's story, and she said thoughtfully, "Brad... remember a while ago you were hooked into the university system? That wouldn't be the same system that stores personnel records on the university staff, would it?"

"No problem." He got up and leaned over her, clearing the screen. "You got any particular personnel record in mind?"

Callie almost giggled with a delicious sense of wickedness. So, Sage McCormick thought he had secrets, did he? "Yes," she told Brad. "McCormick, Sage. Languages Department."

Brad called up the roster for the Languages Department. "Middle initial?"

Callie thought back to her new registration slip. "A," she remembered.

Brad punched in the name.

The screen hesitated for a moment, cleared, and then flashed the annoyed message, "Inaccurate data. Please try again."

"Must be the wrong initial," Brad murmured and entered another code. The screen displayed a listing of all Languages Department personnel, and near the bottom of the list was "McCormick, Sage A. Russian."

Brad tried again and got the same message. "Something's screwed up here," he muttered and brought up a new listing to the screen. "This is everyone on staff here," he explained to her, "their employee ID numbers and social security numbers and payroll numbers. . .they may have switched the entry key for some reason. We can use the numbers to find out."

Brad began talking to the computer with his fingers, and for a while it looked as though the machine would be cooperative. It confirmed that Sage McCormick was indeed on staff, that he had received his last payroll check on the first day of the month, but when Brad tried to call up the personnel file, he was informed by the computer, "Improper Access Code. Try Again."

Brad swore softly and tried again. Obviously he was not used to the computer turning on him. This time the screen printed, McCormick, Sage A. Department, Russian. SS 769-253-8081. ID 76549 8210. And then, incredibly, it began to flash, "File delete. . .File delete. . .File delete. . ."

"Well, that's crazier than hell," Brad murmured, and there was more fascination in his tone than irritation. "How could that happen?"

Callie looked at him uneasily. "What?"

"Somebody's taken this joker's file out of the system." And then to check his theory, he quickly asked for the records of several other staff members at random. They appeared without hesitation. He requested Sage's file and got the same message as before.

Callie, novice that she was, knew this was not a common occurrence. For one thing, she could tell by the look on Brad's face. Why should the one file she asked for be inaccessible? The entire episode was very unsettling, and she wished she had not brought it up.

Brad sat back, studying the screen thoughtfully for a moment, and then he leaned forward and typed out imperiously, "Clarify."

The computer, obviously relieved at being given a command with which it could comply, responded on the screen with "Code 47."

Callie glanced at Brad. "What's that?"

"Code forty-seven," he responded absently, still staring at the computer. "It's the code for authorized entry to the system and approved changes in the program. It lets you know that whatever happened wasn't accidental." He grunted, and it was a sound of amazement and perplexity. "Funny."

"But, why," questioned Callie, "would anyone want to take McCormick's file out?"

He simply shook his head. "I haven't the faintest idea. Whoever it was, though, knew about this system. Code forty-seven is like a secret password. I didn't know anybody connected with the university even knew it."

Callie frowned, both disturbed and disappointed. It appeared Sage was going to be able to keep his secrets after all. "Well," she said in a moment, dismissing it, "thanks for trying anyway. I still think the whole thing is amazing."

He shrugged and sipped from the canned drink. "It's all yours, any time you need it."

But then a sudden thought struck Callie. "But—

isn't this expensive? I mean, shouldn't I pay you for the computer time?''

He grinned, slowly, sweetly, and shook his head so that the sheaf of blond hair bounced gently around his face. He looked at that moment like nothing more than a shy little boy. "Naw, not necessary.''

But Callie was adamant. Within her limited knowledge she was aware that computer networks did cost money, at least as much as a long-distance phone call of the same duration. She said, "No, that's ridiculous. It's going to cost you, and I insist—''

He sat up, lifting innocent eyebrows above green eyes that sparkled with subtle mischief. "But that's just it," he told her. "It doesn't cost me anything.'' As Callie's lips formed a puzzled question, he shrugged in concession. "Okay,'' he agreed. "You can pay me if you like.'' And then his eyes darted to her quickly, almost shyly, but the sparkle within them was irresistible. "You can pay me back by going to a party with me this weekend.''

This was what Callie had been afraid of. Brad was taking her overtures of friendship and interpreting them on a social—maybe even romantic—level. She should have seen it coming. She had thought she had made it clear to him, but apparently she had only been fooling herself. This was awkward, very embarrassing, and she didn't know what to say. She didn't want to hurt his feelings.

Callie turned back to the keyboard, wishing she could push a button to answer this one. She knew no alternative but the truth. "Brad," she said hesitantly. "I appreciate the invitation, I really do..." She glanced at him, sitting cross-legged on the bed in his brown corduroys and Izod shirt, the soft drink cupped beneath his hands, looking vulnerable and sweet and far too hopeful. She really didn't want to hurt his feelings. "I appreciate everything," she added gently, "and I really like you. I want to be your friend, but..."

"But you're afraid I've got a crush on you," Brad supplied easily.

Callie did not know quite how to react to such disarming honesty. She blinked once in amazement, and his grin was back. He shrugged. "Maybe I do." He glanced at her and she saw the teasing glint in his eye. "Or maybe I will. Right now I'm just interested in getting someone to go to this party with me. It's very bad for the image," he confided, "to show up stag."

Callie tried to repress a grin that was as youthful as his. "You don't know any girls your own age?" she challenged.

"Bores." He dismissed them. The sparkle in his eye compelled her even as he lowered his voice to a lewd whisper, "You see, I have this thing for older women..."

Callie laughed. Brad really was adorable. And she did not think he was serious about having a crush on her...at least not yet. She shouldn't be so defensive. "You just remember this older woman is strictly off limits," she told him.

"It's a deal. What about the party Saturday night?"

"I don't know," she evaded, turning back to the keyboard. "How do you turn this thing off?"

Brad bounced to his knees on the bed and set the drink can on the desk beside her. "Make it a date and I'll show you a secret," he persuaded.

She regarded him skeptically. "No date."

"A promise then." What a pretty, dramatically mobile face he had. He could make it express anything from winning persuasion to a childish sulk to worldly wisdom and he never once lost the innocent sparkle that told her it was all in fun.

She shook her head dryly. "I bet you play hell with the hearts of the girls on campus. What's your secret?"

He sprang off the bed and gestured her to relinquish her seat in front of the keyboard. The party was momentarily forgotten in favor of a more interesting game.

She watched him tap out letters on the keyboard, and he inquired, not looking up, "Do you have your checkbook?"

She looked at him for a moment, puzzled, and then retrieved it from her purse. "Why?"

He took the checkbook from her, opened it, and in a moment began typing on the keyboard again.

He sat back with an expansive grin, looking at the screen. "How does it feel to be a millionaire?" he inquired.

Callie peered hesitantly over his shoulder. On the screen was displayed her name, her account number, and a list of all the transactions she had made during the past month. Callie glanced at her checkbook for confirmation and it was all accurate. Except for one thing. The balance on the bottom of her checkbook read $387.42. The balance on the screen read $376,420,000,000.00.

She looked at Brad. "Not funny," she said.

"Sure it is," he contradicted easily. "*This* is not funny." He pressed a button and the screen began to roll. "See," he explained easily, "any fool could catch that as a computer error. You go writing a check for three million on that balance and they'd laugh in your face. However..." His face became intent on the numbers he was punching into the terminal. "First we find an account to cover your check..." More tapping. "Then we make a deposit..." He sat back from the screen. "*Voilà*. Mr. George Williams of Williams and Cale, Stockbrokers, has just written you a check for three hundred seventy six million, four hundred twenty thousand dollars. Your ship has come in."

Callie stared at the screen in a growing sense of wonder and dread, but intermingled with those emotions was something even more dramatic. Power. She told herself it was nothing more than numbers on a screen, altered figures, meaning nothing... But it felt powerful. It felt incredibly powerful.

She said cautiously, "Do you mean if I went to the bank and wrote a check for a million dollars..."

"They wouldn't blink an eye," Brad assured her. Then he admitted, "Well, they might blink an eye—not too many tellers see nine zeros on a check every day of their lives—but they'd have to honor it. They couldn't find any reason not to. The money is there. It belongs to you.''

It took a moment for that to sink in. Callie simply stared.

"Besides," Brad added, "you wouldn't write a check for a million, you'd write it for a thousand. You wouldn't really even want to deposit a million all at one time...you'd take a couple of thousand a week, and all from different accounts and different banks, of course." He shrugged. "Piece of cake."

Callie had heard of such things. She'd never really believed it was possible. Or so easy. She certainly had never expected to see it for herself, right in front of her eyes in glowing green and white. The wonder that had fluttered like butterflies in her stomach knotted into fear, repulsion, a sort of sick awe. Brad suddenly did not seem like an innocent little boy any more. Suddenly she wanted very badly to go home.

"Do you, uh..." She tried to keep her voice steady. "Do this sort of thing often?"

He shrugged. "Sure. Banks are one of the easiest systems in the world to break into. All you've got to do is find the right key."

Power. It was an awesome thing. And this boy, barely out of high school, held it all in his hands. Callie felt slightly queasy.

"Erase it," she said hoarsely.

He looked up at her, and then suddenly his brows flew up in amazement, his eyes crackled mirth.

"Hey," he accused laughing, "you don't think I *keep* it, do you?"

Callie looked at him warily. Her heart was thumping. What had she gotten herself into?

"Don't you?" she inquired, very softly.

Again he laughed. "Hell, no. Who needs it? It's just a game." He tapped out a command and the screen changed. "There," he told her with a flourish. "Reduced to penury again. Happy?"

Callie glanced at the screen, saw that the balance was, indeed, back to normal, and then looked at Brad. She wanted to believe him. He was easy to believe. And that sick feeling was starting to fade away from her stomach. "But if you don't keep it," she began cautiously.

"Look," he said impatiently, hooking his arm over the back of the chair and reaching for his drink, "the only thing I ever steal is computer time, and that's standard operating procedure for hackers. The rest is just for fun. If I had known you were going to get so uptight about it, I never would have shown you."

Callie's mind was whirring. She tried to think of the implications, but they were too much for her. Everything from medical records to payrolls was in some way linked to computers. Income tax records, criminal trials, newspaper stories, telephone calls...air traffic control, insurance files, top-secret research, the national defense system... This boy, or someone like him, could push a button and begin the economic collapse of the entire free world. He could launch a missile or crash a plane or

wipe out the navigational systems of ships at sea...
The thought tingled through her with horror and
dread. Power. He held the key that controlled the
world.

No. She was being overly dramatic. She had been
watching too many movies, reading too many sci-fi
novels. It wasn't that easy in real life. It just
couldn't be.

And in the end, through all the rubble that was
crashing and spinning in her mind, Callie picked up
on only one word. "Hackers?" she repeated carefully.

Brad nodded, draining the last of his drink.
"Computer freaks. It's like a secret organization.
You know, a kind of club or..." He shrugged. "I
don't know. It's just something that guys who are
really into computers do. We try to break the systems just to see if we can do it. The harder they are,
the more fun it is to get into. Sometimes we com-
pete with each other to see who's best... sometimes
we help each other out."

Again he shrugged rather defensively. "Hell, it's
just a game. We don't take anything, or do anything wrong... Too much bad stuff can come
down if you get caught." But then the irrepressible
grin of self-conscious pride broke through and he
added, "Sometimes we leave a little sign that we got
through—like 'Kilroy was here.'" There was something about that—Kilroy was here—that struck a
familiar, uneasy chord in Callie, but she couldn't
remember what it was. And Brad was talking so fast
that she had enough to do to concentrate on what

he was saying. "It freaks the guys out on the other end of the system to find out an 'amateur' broke into a program they thought was fail-safe. But," he told her, defensive again, "nothing worse than that. It's just for fun, you know."

There was a vulnerable expression in his eyes, beyond the cockiness, that practically pleaded with her not to judge him. Callie knew she should say something stern and reprimanding; she knew what he was doing was wrong and her own sense of morality should have been insulted. But her conscience was buried deep beneath her fascination, and though she was ashamed of it, she had to question, "Can you—break into any system in the world?"

He laughed, relaxing a little now that he saw she was not upset with him. Callie was even more disgusted with herself. She was encouraging his delinquency. "Hardly!" Brad answered. "I know all the doomsday people are claiming the fate of the world hinges on computers. One slip on the keyboard and we all go up in smoke... But the fact is most systems are pretty damn secure. And they're getting more secure now that there are more people like me learning how to break in faster than they can put up the locks...which only makes it more of a challenge, of course, and more fun when we do make it. University systems, of course, are unsecured," he continued, warming to the subject.

Callie had the feeling Brad was desperately trying to placate her, to impress her beyond the point where she would be disapproving or angry. Just like a little boy bringing his mother flowers after a spanking. "And like I said, banks—but that could change any day now. They're starting to realize how vulnerable they are, but nothing in the world moves slower than a bunch of bankers, unless. . ." And he grinned. "It's the government." He was really getting excited now, squirming in his chair, a lecturer filled with more information than he could possibly impart in a limited amount of time. "It's true," he insisted. "US government systems are a piece of cake—mostly because the computers they use are so outdated. I'm not talking about defense system stuff," he assured her quickly. "That's just for pulp magazines and cheap movies. . .there are so many backups and fail-safe features on the war department systems that even if you could crack it, it wouldn't do any good." And again he grinned. "Not that it hasn't been tried. I mean other stuff—payroll records, promotions, Treasury Department, FBI—everything that's on the old computers."

Again something stirred in the back of Callie's mind. She squelched it quickly and sternly. This was wrong. It was immoral if not illegal. . .she shouldn't be standing here listening to this. . . But said, "Do you mean you can open up even top-secret FBI files—from here?"

He nodded. "All you have to do is find the right password."

"What," inquired Callie cautiously, "if you can't?"

Brad shrugged. "I usually can. Me, or someone

else in the network. You just have to learn to think like these guys, that's all.''

This is wrong. Callie thought very clearly. Don't you know how much influence you have on this boy? Don't you see what big trouble he's heading for? Don't you care? "Brad..." she said slowly. "Something just struck me. A friend of mine—he's a reporter—is doing a story on some famous underground characters of the sixties. If I gave you a list..."

"Hey, no problem," he responded immediately. He was delighted. "There's nothing this baby can't do." He patted the computer terminal fondly.

Quickly, before she lost her courage, Callie wrote down three names on a scrap of paper on the desk. Two of them, she knew already from Jerry's research, were dead. The middle name was Jed Frye.

She was disgusted with herself.

Brad took up the paper. Maybe it was a testament to the generation gap that he did not recognize any of the names. "I'll let you know as soon as I get something," he promised. Then he looked up at her, smiling. "So how about that party?"

Callie's smile was a little weak. "Sure. Why not?"

Brad's joy with her answer almost made up for her betrayal of him.

She walked alone across the busy bright campus, the pumpkin-harvest colors of the sparkling afternoon a perfect counterpoint for her mood. Shame and excitement mingled in her stomach and crept through her veins like an illegal drug. Her mind

raced; her spirits darkened. Breaking into an FBI
file...was she crazy? Was *Brad* crazy? She had
stood there and watched him rob banks and listened
to him confess computer fraud and not once had
she raised a single objection. Not once had she
thought of anything much beyond her own self interest.

Callie was using Brad, just like she had used
Jerry, just like she had used anyone and everyone
else who happened to cross her path, and all of it to
further a single goal...a single chase whose prize
was probably nothing... She hated herself for it,
but she couldn't stop it. She thought about what
Sage had said the other night, about the legacy of
wanderlust her father had given her. Could such
things as morality and social responsibility also be
inherited?

"Oh Daddy," she whispered miserably to herself, and tipped her face up helplessly toward the
sun. "What have you done to me?"

Chapter Six

"Miss Lester!"

Only when she heard the running clip of steps behind her did Callie realize that her name had been called—and more than once. She turned quickly and was face to face with Sage McCormick.

"Not the best way to start off a relationship," he informed her with a dry lift of his eyebrow, drawing up beside her. "Especially when you consider I'm doing you a favor."

Callie simply looked at him in confusion, and he gave a resigned shake of his head. "Tuesday afternoon?" he prompted. "Three o'clock, my office?"

"Oh, no." The moan was drawn from Callie involuntarily, and she flushed with chagrin. "The lessons! I forgot."

"Obviously." His fingers closed lightly around her elbow and he nodded toward a spot across the lawn. "You have exactly one hour and twenty minutes to redeem yourself."

The touch of his fingers on her elbow was warm and rejuvenating; his scent was as woodsy and fresh as the crisp autumn day surrounding them. The sight of him was a balm to her troubled spirit, and his very presence was like being lifted out of an uncertain netherworld of corruption and into a place that was real and bright and clean. Even the amused annoyance that flashed in his face was reassuring. It surprised Callie...what he could do to her. He made her feel good just by being near.

He led her across the springy grass, which had not yet been wilted by a killing frost, and toward the spindly shadows of a partially denuded maple tree. The landscape maintenance crew was very meticulous, and the falling leaves were diligently swept away every day. Beneath the tree was nothing but an inviting bed of grass, and it was there that Sage gestured her to be seated.

"If you don't mind," he added, and he spread his leather jacket on the ground. "Seems a shame to waste all this sunshine—there won't be too many days of it left."

Callie did not mind in the least. Sitting in the sun with him for an hour or two promised to be the only good thing that had happened to her all day and it would be wonderful to just lean back and relax and let her problems drift away in the quiet, undemanding comfort of his presence... What was she thinking? Russian, that was all he was interested in and all she should be interested in. And it was the last thing in the world she felt like concentrating on.

Callie hesitated, then she untied the sleeves of her cardigan from around her neck and spread it on the ground beside his jacket. She had been shopping over the weekend, and her heather-toned skirt and cowl-necked sweater were just as fashionable as she could wish. The matching cardigan was an affectation Tandy had added to her apparel at the last minute this morning, but now Callie was grateful she had. "The ground will be just as cold for you as it is for me," she explained to Sage and sank down on top of her sweater.

He cocked her a wry look. "How gallant of you," he murmured, but took her advice and sat on his jacket.

His denim-clad knee was very close to hers, and Callie unobtrusively moved hers away on the pretense of straightening her skirt. But as she did, he shifted position, reaching for his briefcase, and their thighs brushed. When he settled his weight again, their legs remained in close contact, barely touching, but seeming to Callie as intimate and explicit as a nude embrace. But he did not seem to notice the contact, and Callie tried not to draw attention to it by moving away.

Today, Sage was dressed in a long-sleeved camouflage overshirt that was unbuttoned and untucked over a gray T-shirt that advertised Moosehead Beer. The soft cotton undergarment hugged the contours of his chest and drew attention to a spare abdomen, where an ornately carved brass buckle nestled between denim and leather. The lines of his jeans swept down over slim hips and taut thighs in one unbroken contour, tenting a little in his lap as he brought one booted foot to rest against his inner thigh in a semi-lotus position.

Callie quickly jerked her eyes away. What was she doing? What did it matter to her how he was dressed? Why should she care how sexy he looked in the trendy, casual attire, nor how comfortable he made her feel sitting there beside her on the grass, exuding the fragrances of leather and sunshine and crackling autumn foliage... She was annoyed with herself and, inexplicably, with him. And the last thing she felt like doing was studying Russian.

As she reached for a notepad and pen from her own stack of books, a sudden, crisp breeze swept across the lawn, dislodging the papers in Sage's open briefcase. They both reached to anchor them at once, and their hands touched.

The fingers of Sage's hand tightened warmly over hers while papers flapped and rustled wildly beneath their weight. Their eyes met, and he was smiling, a coaxing light kindling in the back of his eyes. "Now you see why I like to work outside?" he suggested. "First a little hand holding, then you'll get chilly and I'll have to put my arm around you..."

Callie removed her hand, then grabbed quickly for a paper that was jerked away by a second breeze. She glanced at it for a moment before returning it to him, just to give herself a moment to bring the conversation back onto a professional level, and then something caught her attention.

The paper she had grabbed was a pulpy newsletter called "New Freedom," not unlike the supermarket scandal sheets, except the contents of this one were much more serious. And more dangerous.

A headline read, "Political Corruption Seeping into Private Sector," and another, "Government Control of Airways Revealed," and another, "Free Enterprise Threatens Free Choice." Callie scanned with a growing sense of repulsion a few lines here and there. "How much longer," it questioned, "will we tolerate this sham of a democracy? Is this what our Founding Fathers envisioned?" "Murmured objections are no longer enough..." "Revolution is the principle upon which this country was established..." " 'Let them eat cake' is the cry from Washington today... The present administration should take a lesson from history before it finds itself facing its own Reign of Terror..." "Blood will flow in the streets..." "Plowshares beaten into swords..."

It was scary.

"What," inquired Callie, slowly returning the paper to him, "is this?"

Sage took it from her, his expression implacable. "Just another handout from another radical group. You'll find them all over the campus."

Callie felt that uneasy sense of corruption, of ugliness, steal over her again. "It sounds... violent," she ventured.

Sage appeared to be watching her very carefully behind a face that was still unerringly neutral. "They have some valid points," he answered. "And the one thing that the government hasn't yet succeeded in taking away from us is the freedom of self-expression."

Callie tried not to be shocked. He had a right to

his opinion; it was just that she had been in too many countries where this sort of propaganda was the only truth the public knew and the streets really had run with blood....

As though reading her thoughts, Sage commented nonchalantly, folding a crease into the newspaper, "You've been in places where you've seen firsthand what happens when government repression takes over. You should be able to sympathize with feelings like these."

A whisper of a breeze, much lighter than the ones that had gone before it, traced a cold finger across Callie's cheek, and she shivered. Was she imagining things, or was Sage trying to draw her out into a discussion of radical politics? And why did that disturb her so? It didn't matter to Callie what Sage's politics were; it was none of her business. She remembered what she had done less than a half hour ago in that cluttered dormitory room with Brad, and she knew she had no right to pass judgment on anyone. She didn't even want to think about it.

She took out her textbook without glancing at him again. "Where do we start?" she suggested.

But Callie couldn't help thinking about it. The mysteries of the Russian alphabet were lost upon her; the letters danced like hieroglyphics before her eyes against the background of her own jumbled thoughts. Well, what else was she supposed to do? she tried to defend herself. Brad had presented her with a heaven-sent opportunity and was she supposed to just turn her back on it? Brad could find out in a matter of hours what it would take Jerry years to do—if ever. And Jerry wasn't being particularly cooperative of late either, come to think of it. At the very least she might be able to find out what made Jerry's source think Jed Frye had ended up on this campus in the first place, and then she would at least know where to start looking.

And it wasn't as though Jerry himself had not forced a few locks in his time...sometimes the only way to find out the truth was to tread the fine line between lawful and criminal activity. And she had searched so long, she was getting so tired. She deserved to take a few shortcuts.

It wasn't as though she had corrupted Brad's morals...he was used to breaking and entering via computer, and he would have continued to do so whether or not she had come into his life. And it wasn't as though they were taking anything—except perhaps the secret that would untangle her whole life and let her rest in peace at last.

Sage closed the textbook, capturing her fingers between the pages, and Callie looked up, startled. His expression was gently mocking. "It wasn't *that* bad."

Callie was lost. "What?"

"The filthy joke I just told you in Russian."

Callie laughed nervously and pulled her trapped fingers out of the book. "Sorry, I missed it. Was it funny?"

"I thought it was hilarious." He took her book and the notepad and pen that rested in her lap and put them on top of his briefcase. "However, there's no accounting for taste I suppose." And he looked at her. "What's wrong?"

Callie quickly glanced away, busily brushing a scrap of grass off her skirt. When she looked into those patiently inquisitive eyes, she could easily imagine herself telling him anything, everything. . . And it would feel so good to tell someone. "Just because I don't laugh at dirty jokes—"

Unexpectedly Sage touched her chin with his forefinger, tilting her face to look at him. Callie knew she was lost. "Just because," he corrected, "the last time I saw you those great big eyes were sparkling and dancing like diamond chips. . ."

"The last time you saw me," Callie protested uncomfortably, moving her face only slightly to break the contact with his finger, "I was drunk." His touch left a warm imprint on her chin, a memory of something incredibly soft and tingling that took a long time to fade away.

"And now," he continued, ignoring her interruption, "they look like the North Atlantic when a storm is brewing. So what's going on in that troubled little head of yours?"

Eyes as clear as an autumn sky, strong face composed and relaxed, his posture easy and unhurried, his tone inviting. . . Sage should have been a priest, Callie thought. Everything about him was persuasion to confession, and whenever Callie was around him, she wanted to pour out her soul.

She sighed, her eyes skating away from his and above to the colorful cornucopia of changing leaves interspersed with cobalt sky, and she said softly,

"Oh...Lord." Why fight it? She needed to tell someone, she would be miserable until she did. But why did he always seem to make the telling so easy? Callie glanced at him hesitantly, then down at the ground again, shrugging her shoulders uncomfortably under the weight of her guilt. "I just did something very wrong," she said, "and I'm ashamed of myself."

Sage contemplated this thoughtfully. "I assume you had good reason," he said in a moment.

"The same old reason," she answered, almost to herself. Her fingers absently plucked up blades of springlike grass, shredded them, and let them fall. "The same reason that's been pushing and pulling me all my life..." Callie stopped, knowing that that could not possibly make any sense to him, and knowing he probably could not care less. How did he do this to her? She was constantly reminding herself that she had known him less than a week, though when she was with him it seemed as though he had been around forever, had seen her through all her crises, had advised her on all her choices, and knew all her secrets...

Callie thought Sage would question her unfinished statement, but he chose another tactic. "This—'wrong' thing you did," he inquired. "Was it illegal or immoral?"

Why should she answer that? It was just that he was so natural and nonjudgmental that her aching conscience had no choice. She sighed again. "Both," she answered heavily.

"Hmm." He looked at her for a moment,

thoughtfully. Still there was absolutely no sign of condemnation or accusation in his face. And then he simply asked, "What are your chances of getting caught?"

Her eyes flew to his in surprise and shocked suspicion, and very slowly, he smiled. She saw the gentle teasing in his eyes that advised her to stop taking herself so seriously. "Lighten up," he said. "Nothing can be that bad." And then, suddenly, he grabbed her hand, pulling her to her feet. "As a matter of fact," he announced, "I can't think of any ill in the world a hot fudge sundae can't cure, and you look as though you're in bad need of just that prescription."

Callie couldn't help laughing as he tugged her into step with him, stumbling a little and protesting, "But—what about our lesson? And our books?" She gestured over her shoulder. "We can't just leave them here!"

"The lesson can wait," he dismissed it, "and if anyone wants my Russian text or yesterday's test papers, they're welcome to them."

Callie laughed and let the weight of her problems evaporate into his carefree mood.

They went to an ice cream shop across the street, where Sage ordered two hot fudge sundaes with double portions of whipped cream and chopped nuts on top. The interior was not very crowded this time of day—most of the students had already headed for the pizza place—and they found a booth in the corner near the window. Callie hadn't done anything like this since...she had to think back, and she couldn't remember that far.

She couldn't believe how quickly the confusion of the afternoon evaporated into the slick, rich taste of fudge and melting ice cream, how the presence of one easygoing and slightly avant-garde man across the table from her could make her feel young again when, in fact, she had never really been young at all. Was the fact that she could so easily forget her moral transgressions of only a few hours ago yet another sign of her asocial tendencies? Callie didn't know, and right now she didn't care. Right now all she was interested in was the way the slanting sunlight fell through the dusty windowpane and sprinkled silver in Sage's curls, turning one side of his face to golden, leaving the other in shadows. Right now she would have been pleased to think of nothing and do nothing but pretend they were no more than two people eating ice cream on a Tuesday afternoon...two people who were young and almost innocent, unspoiled by experience or disappointment or worldly wisdom, two people who were maybe even just a little in love...

The smile she caught in Sage's eyes when she looked up briefly embarrassed and flustered her a little. It was slow and gentle, and it made her feel as though he had read verbatum the wispy fantasy that was floating through her head—and that he approved. But his next words dispelled that unsettling impression, and she was relieved. He said, "It's your father, isn't it?"

Callie swallowed quickly, dropping her eyes for a moment, wondering where that had come from. She touched her napkin to her lips and glanced at him. "What is?"

He dipped his spoon into the dish, scooping up gooey fudge and ice cream, and his nonchalant manner relaxed her. "Whatever's bothering you. The motivation behind the illegal and immoral thing you just did."

Still, Callie was cautious. She flattened out a mound of whipped cream with the back of her spoon. "What makes you think that?"

Sage smiled at her, hesitating before he brought the spoon to his lips. "You're pretty transparent. You said 'the same old reason' and it wasn't hard to figure out that looking for your father must have motivated you most of your life."

Callie looked at him soberly as he slid the spoon into his mouth, and he did not flinch from her gaze. Did he have any idea what a relief it was to be able to talk to someone about it, to have someone understand without being told the biggest secret and the biggest pain in her life... She nodded slowly and began to push the ice cream around in her dish. "Right," she agreed softly. Then she smiled a little self-consciously, trying to force a note of lightness into her tone which she was far from feeling. "As a matter of fact," she told Sage, "that's how I ended up on this campus. I was planning to go back to school anyway," she explained, "but I got word that—well, that my father might be here somewhere, and..." She shrugged, trailing off. It sounded lame even to her own ears. Was she such a single-minded child? Was she really allowing her life to be ruled to such a great extent by this hopeless cause?

But Sage did not appear to think her reasons for being here either childish or hopeless. In fact he only seemed interested. "That shouldn't be too hard to check out," he volunteered. "Why don't you let me help?"

Callie looked at him, and her amazement and gratitude were in her eyes. Just like that. "Let me help..." Probably the most beautiful words in the English language. He was concerned, he was involved, he cared. And the temptation to let him help was enormous. Was there anything he could do? If she told him the truth, if she confessed her dilemma, could he somehow make her search easier? She knew that merely the telling and the sharing of her burden would make it easier, and she wanted more than anything at that moment to tell Sage the truth.

The truth. That her father was a notorious terrorist, a murderer, a felon, a fugitive from justice... Callie shrank from the possibility. To tell Sage and watch that warm light fade from his eyes, to tell Sage and feel him draw away from her into suspicion and distance... And suddenly Callie knew that above all else, that she could not bear. She did not want Sage to know. She wanted to keep him and the small part of her life he occupied clear of corruption and untainted by the past. Callie did not want to know what Sage would think of her if he found out she was the daughter of Jed Frye.

So she merely smiled, looked down at the mushy milkshake she had made of her sundae, and shook her head helplessly. "It was a good idea," she said, referring to the ice cream, "but I'm afraid I blew it. Look at this mess."

His gentle smile told her that he understood the double meaning of her words, and he would not push. He reached for her hand as he stood up.

They did not turn back toward the campus but walked in the opposite direction down a quiet tree-lined street that sheltered stately stone homes. The sun was fading into a muted gray-green glow and the oranges and browns of the foliage overhead were dying with the light into shadows of their former glory. The air was still and fragrant, holding just a hint of the day's warmth as it waited for night to steal the last rays of the sun and spread its frosty breath over the dormant landscape. The only sound was the crunching carpet of dried leaves beneath their feet, and Sage held Callie's hand.

The silence was easy and comforting, their linked hands an unspoken expression of natural rapport. Callie tried to understand it but she could not... She was comfortable with Sage. She felt at home with him. She knew nothing about him. They had only known one another for a few days, meeting briefly for an hour or two at a time. They had talked about very little of substance within those brief hours together, yet it almost seemed as though there was no need to. It almost seemed as though they understood more of one another from what was not said than from what was spoken. Callie felt close to him, and perhaps the very fact that she could not understand it was what made it so.

"This is my favorite time of year," Sage said

after a while, quietly. He looked up into the trees, breathed deeply of the woodsy air, and then smiled—not at her, but at the world in general. "Days like this always make me feel like falling in love."

A surprised tingle coursed through her with the unexpected sensitivity of that statement—not a pass, not an innuendo directed at Callie—just an easy expression of sentiment. And Callie knew what he meant. There was something vibrant and compelling about autumn that stirred the emotions, a final and flamboyant display of the energy of life before winter's long dormancy. Colors were more brilliant, scents keener, tastes sharper, and every sense in Callie's body responded to it. She had never known anyone else who felt the same way.

The shiver that passed through her was of pleasure and wonder, but Sage interpreted it as a sign of cold and slipped his arm around her shoulders. Callie was not sorry. "Have you ever been married, Callie?" he asked.

She was neither surprised by nor on guard against the turn of the conversation. She shook her head against the curve of his arm. "No." And she glanced up at him. "Have you?"

The smile that curved downward on his lips might very well have been bitter. "Hardly!" He seemed to speak without thinking, as though he were telling her something she already knew. "In my line of work, it never seemed quite fair."

Callie was puzzled, for she could think of no more stable or promising profession than that of a language professor, and she could not understand why Sage would consider his line of work "unfair" to anyone concerned. But before she could question, he abruptly changed the subject.

"You said it was your father—or looking for him—that brought you here," Sage commented. "Does that mean you're not planning to go for a degree after all? That if your search doesn't pan out, you'll be moving on?"

Callie was thoughtful for a moment before answering. It felt so good just walking with him, just being with him in the filtering evening light and imagining that they had known each other forever, that there was nothing they could not discuss. Usually Callie found it awkward to walk with a man while his arm was around her, but Sage was the perfect height for her. She fit neatly against him and their steps were evenly matched. They flowed together in movement so naturally that Callie could not help wondering what it would be like to dance with him, to feel the full length of his body against hers, to be wrapped in his arms and feel his face next to hers. . .

She said carefully "No. That's not what I meant at all. This thing with my father—it's really more of a habit than anything else, I guess. Or a hobby. I know the chances of my ever finding him are pretty much nil, and I can't let my whole life revolve around it."

She knew he wanted to say something—perhaps she felt it in the quickening of his muscles or heard the small intake of his breath—but he restrained himself. Their footsteps echoed and rustled on the pavement beneath them, and Callie was cold everywhere except where Sage's arm encircled her. There she was toasty warm.

She said after a time, "Do you always dress like that?"

He glanced at her in amused surprise. "Like what?"

Callie felt a tingle of warmth steal into her cheeks. Despite the intimacy that had evolved between them within the space of the afternoon, she was not quite certain she wanted to guide the conversation onto an even more personal level. Somehow commenting on his clothing seemed to be an admission of the physical attraction she felt for him and she was sure he knew it.

She shrugged against the warm muscle of his arm, but could think of no way to get out of it now. "Like a hippie," she said.

He laughed. "Now that phrase dates both of us, doesn't it? I haven't heard that in years—not since I was one."

She looked up at him, curious. "You were?"

His eyes still held a twinkle in the fading light and one eyebrow was twisted dryly. "The less said about those days, the better," he answered. "So you think my attire is unprofessional, do you?"

She was no longer embarrassed; she was, in fact, warming to the subject. He had a way of making her do that. "It just doesn't seem very professor—ish," she agreed.

"Hmm." He appeared to take her opinion under

thoughtful consideration. "Well," he offered, "I suppose I could point out that the kids I teach aren't exactly three-piece suiters themselves and it's important to be able to relate to them on their level..."

"Makes sense," Callie allowed.

"And that it helps to be able to blend into the crowd at exam time when disappointed students are likely to throw bricks..."

Callie giggled.

"But the truth of the matter is," Sage informed her, "one of the advantages of being a Russian professor is that you're allowed to be eccentric. And I make it a policy to take every advantage I can get."

Something had softened in his voice with the last, and Callie could feel his eyes upon her. Their steps slowed as Callie turned her face to look at him, and everything stilled within her body in quiet anticipation as their eyes met. His face was shadowed, but his eyes a clear glow, gently intense. She felt his fingers tighten on hers just slightly, and slowly he brought their linked hands upward so that his fist rested against her cheek. He released one long forefinger to trace the shadow of her temple, a butterfly touch that made her shiver. And he kept looking at her, thoughtfully, tenderly. She felt the rhythm of her heart respond to the message in his eyes. Her fingers moved against his involuntarily, anxious for the freedom to touch his face as he did hers.

He said softly, "I wonder what would happen if I pressed my advantage now?"

Callie did not know what made her say it. "Try,"

she whispered, and his face moved toward hers.

Her lips were parted and breathless as they met his, and the softness of the touch surprised her. Surprised her, then weakened her, then started a warmth inside her that spread like a flame on dry kindling, fanned by the gradually increasing pressure of his lips on hers until her body felt like a beacon that glowed and radiated heat in the cold stillness of the night. His fingers opened against her face, trapping her own hand between her cheek and his palm, and she could feel the pulse of heat that seemed to leap from his hand, through hers, to her face, then deeper, burning gradually to the center of her brain.

Callie's knees weakened; she swayed against him. Her hand touched his waist for support and felt the heat radiate from flesh beneath the smooth fabric of his T-shirt. His fingers circled against her spine, drawing her closer. His muscles tensed, and there was a catch in his breath as his mouth opened upon hers, drawing her deeper, demanding more.

Callie had not expected this. She had not imagined that the mild attraction she had felt for him could flare into such a brilliant sexual awareness, that the taste of him and the feel of him would start a hunger that grew more mindless by the minute, that the power of one kiss could strip her so completely and draw every cell of her body into a pulsing need for him... It was too fast, too overwhelming, too unexpected...

Sage's fingers threaded through her hair, and her hand slipped weakly to rest against his forearm as

he tilted her head to follow the tasting motions of
his tongue and his lips. Callie could feel the strain in
the muscle of his arm, feel the unsteady brush of
warm breath on her cheek. He had not expected this
either, and she could sense the surprise and wonder
within him that persuaded him to pull back even as
his instincts urged him to push forward. Callie's
fingers tightened on his arm; she tried to move her
face in protest but everything within her rebelled.
She wanted to be touched by him, to touch him and
hold him and let nature take them where it would,
but a thin voice of reason cried out to her to stop, to
move away before this got too far out of hand . . .

And Sage responded to even so weak a signal. His
lips gradually left hers, clasping gently, stroking
and caressing, moving lightly to her cheek where the
heat of his breath was a tingling contrast to the chill
breeze that had begun to dry the sheen of moisture
from her face. And all the while his arms were tightening around her, drawing her into a secure embrace full length against his body. The thumping of
his chest was steady and hard and it vibrated
throughout Callie's body.

Her hands rested against Sage's shoulders; her
cheek felt the warmth and softness of his T-shirt.
Her breathing was unsteady and her own heart was
still tripping and cavorting uncertainly in her chest.
She was dazed, incapable of analyzing or question-
ing the experience that had just shaken her so pro-
foundly. It shouldn't have been like this. She had
not been prepared for this. But she could have
stood there in the shelter of his arms forever.

And then she felt his face move against her hair. He whispered, "Callie..."

She knew what he was going to say. She knew what he was going to ask, for she wanted it, too. She knew if he said the words, if she saw the question in his eyes, she would be lost. She could not let this happen to her. Not now, not yet, and not with him...

Callie shook her head against his shoulder. She was too weak to step away and give meaning to her refusal. "No," she said simply. It was a husky, breathless syllable, and it sounded no more convincing than it was meant.

Sage's hand came up to touch her chin lightly, turning her face upward to him. There was no reprimand in his face, no accusation for the lie she had just told. He would accept it without question, knowing it was insincere, because the mute plea in her eyes asked him to. His smile was gentle, his eyes as subtle and as clear as starlight, and Callie thought quite clearly, *I could fall in love with this man.*

That she could not afford.

"I think," she said softly, and his thumb caressed her cheek, "we might have discovered something special."

Perhaps he could see the struggle in her eyes. Callie would never know how she managed to smile and make herself move a step away. The lightness of her tone was strained, and her voice was a little unsteady. "Maybe," she suggested, "it's just that time of year. Something in the air that makes you feel like falling in love."

Once again Sage recognized and responded to her unspoken need. His finger stroked her cheek one last time before falling away. "Could be," he agreed. The smile in his eyes was gently teasing; the slight upward curve of his just-kissed lips made a pulse jerk in Callie's throat again. "Or..." His fingers trailed down her arm and linked again lightly with hers. "It could be," he suggested softly, "that I really like you, and I want to be your friend."

Callie had to swallow hard. Everything within her wanted to let that slowly tightening pressure in his hand draw her into his arms again, to melt into him and let him take her where he would... And she said, somewhat hoarsely, "That's all?"

Sage's other hand brushed lightly along the plane of her shoulder blade, tracing the roundness of her shoulder and the delicacy of her upper arm. His eyes held her, his hand caressed her, and she shivered. His expression was very tender. "Not necessarily," he answered. It sounded like a promise, and promises were one thing Callie had a great deal of trouble accepting... or giving.

She dropped her eyes; she turned away. It was almost full night now, and the streetlamps shed a limited mercury-vapor radiance against the still, gray twilight. Their glow was almost as cold as the night that threatened them. Callie took a breath and squared her shoulders and even managed a little smile. "We'd better get back," she said.

That was not what she wanted to say, but other things called her. This time she could not afford to deviate from the path, she could not afford to be distracted, she could not turn back. She was too close.

She hoped Sage understood.

That night Callie had the dream again. The cold, misty street down which she trudged looked very much like the street she and Sage had walked earlier, but this time she was alone. She was alone and tired, and home was just a few steps away; she could see the glow of the windows and smell the smoke from the chimney and with every step the ache inside her grew. Home, home...her steps echoed the refrain, and anticipation swelled within her until she was standing before the door, twisting the knob...

And this time as she was searching frantically for her key, trying not to let the despair overwhelm her, the door swung slowly open from the inside. A shadowy figure filled the threshold, bathed in a golden glow, welcoming her, beckoning her inside. And just as Callie was about to see the face on the figure, she woke up.

She knew she was very close.

Chapter Seven

It seemed since Callie spent most of her time in the library as it was, she usually was glad to see the last of the place. But today she lingered, pretending not to glance at her watch every five minutes, hoping that she would forget that at three o'clock this afternoon she had an appointment with Professor Sage McCormick.

In class yesterday he had not looked her way once, and she had not gone out of her way to attract his attention. He conducted his advanced class in Russian in the same relaxed and enthralling manner as he did the beginning one, joking with the students and inviting audience participation, but never once did his attention stray to Callie. At first she was piqued, for she could have used some special attention in that class—*professional* attention, she assured herself quickly—and it seemed only natural that Sage, having gone to all the trouble of transferring her to a class above her expertise, would want to keep a close eye on her progress. Callie certainly had not expected him to ignore her. But then she was relieved. Perhaps he, too, had come to see the folly of becoming involved with a student, perhaps he had taken her hint the other night that her life was too complicated at present to admit him into it, perhaps he had even forgotten the entire episode... Callie had no doubt that such things must happen to him frequently. It would certainly be easier on both of them if they could keep their relationship on a professional level, and if her feelings were a little hurt now, it was nothing more than pride.

And all of that, of course, was no reason for her to try to avoid another private lesson in Russian. She needed the extra help, not to mention the fact that she was obligated to finish the course... She scowled in annoyance with herself as she gathered up her books. She had five minutes to make it across campus to Sage's office and, all else aside, she would not have him think she was avoiding him. She could be professional, if he could not, and she would make it very plain...

A chirpy voice behind her said, "Where's the fire?"

Callie cast a glance over her shoulder and slowed her steps as Tandy drew up beside her. "Well, this is the last place I expected to run into *you*," Callie replied in low amusement, mindful of the students in the library who had looked up in annoyance at the sound of Tandy's voice.

The younger woman grinned and lowered her own tone to a pitch comparable with Callie's. "Got to keep up appearances, you know." Then she grimaced and cast a covert glance around the room, "Actually," she confided, "this place gives me the creeps. All these books." She shuddered. "Let's get out of here."

Callie giggled. Her roommate was becoming more tolerable every day, although a great part of that might have been because they rarely saw each other. Callie planned her study time for the library when she knew Tandy was going to be home, but the time she did spend in her roommate's company was amusing and relaxing. Callie had finally set the rules about bedtime, and though Tandy pouted a little, she was quite cooperative about keeping the radio volume low after midnight. And since Sage had changed Callie's class schedule, breakfast was one meal Callie gratefully slept through. The two women were rarely ever at home together during the day, and it was working out quite well.

Tandy stretched her short legs to keep up with Callie's rushed stride, and as they stepped out into the chill sunlight, she panted, "What *is* your hurry? This place is going to be here awhile yet, you know!" Then a shrewd look passed over the younger girl's face, and the grin she shot at Callie was both mischievous and superior. "Of course, I remember now!" she declared. "Thursday afternoon—a rendezvous with Professor Gorgeous! No wonder you're in such a rush. I wouldn't keep *him* waiting myself."

Callie was tired of trying to explain to Tandy that there was nothing more between her and Sage than the Russian alphabet, especially since her protestations had begun to run a little hollow of late. She was grateful for the distraction when she had to swerve sharply to avoid a collision with a man who was coming up the steps on the same side they were going down.

She murmured an apology, and then stopped, smiling. "Professor Chalmers," she said, turning to face him as he moved by her, "I hope the coffee stains came out of your coat."

He looked at her, clearly puzzled, for just a moment. Callie knew he did not remember her, but she did not mind, because the smile that slowly lightened his foggy gray eyes pretended that he did. "Oh, yes, my dear," he assured her abstractedly, "Quite all right, good as new. You have a nice day, too, now."

Callie could not help chuckling a little as he wandered away. . . in the opposite direction in which he had originally been headed.

Tandy frowned a little, hugging her books to her chest. "What a spooky old man. Do you know him?"

"Only to bump into," Callie responded with a shrug. "Why? Do you?"

"I interviewed as his lab assistant," responded Tandy. "He told me I had the attention span of a laboratory mouse. He's weird."

Callie smothered a giggle and reflected that that observation hardly qualified the eminent professor as "weird," but she only defended mildly, "I think he has the kindest eyes I've ever seen."

"Maybe," was Tandy's disgruntled reply, "but

everything else about him is weird." Then, in another one of her lightning flashes of mood, she said,
"I'm making yogurt crunch for dinner. See you
then!"

And she was gone before Callie could think of an
excuse to miss dinner.

Callie was six minutes late for her lesson, but she
was relieved that Sage was not ready for her. She
burst into his office without knocking and surprised
him in the midst of an apparently very intense conversation with a dark-haired young man in droopy
mustache... Callie was certain it was the same
youth who had approached Sage that night he had
walked her home after pizza. Both conversers broke
off short at her unexpected entry, and she had the
distinct impression that she had interrupted something very private—an impression that was only
underscored by the quick flash of anger in Sage's
eyes before he arranged a mask of impassivity over
his face. And the other man's expression was un-
mistakable—it was pure alarm, followed by a shaft
of something so swift and dangerous that Callie
automatically took a step backward.

"I—I'm sorry," she stammered. "I—should
have knocked." Her eyes went from the young man
with the curly hair to Sage, and she knew she was
not imagining the tension in the room. She felt as
though she had just walked into a top-secret Security Council meeting and was at any moment now going to be shot as a spy. "I'll come back later," she
said quickly and turned to go.

"Don't be silly, Callie." Sage's voice was relaxed

and natural. "You're late as it is. I was beginning to think you weren't going to show. Come on in and let's get started."

Callie hesitated at the door, but the young man merely gave Sage a silent look that Callie could not read and turned to cross the room. The time he paused before her could not have been more than a few seconds, but his look took in every detail of her, memorizing and storing it with the cold precision of an automatic camera. His eyes were as black as night, and his scrutiny started a clammy feeling in the pit of Callie's stomach. She was glad when he left the room without a word.

Callie glanced after him uncertainly, still a little disturbed by the entire incident. "Wasn't—wasn't that the young man I saw you with the other night?" she ventured as she came into the room. Female curiosity burned within her to know what they could have been discussing to put those looks of alarm and anger on their faces when she interrupted.

Sage was clearing off his desk, and he responded absently, "No, I don't think so. He's just one of my students, here to complain about his grades."

Callie opened her mouth to protest, then shut it again. She had been in both of Sage's classes, and she knew that particular young man was not in either of them. And she *knew* it was the same man who had stepped out of the shadows to confront Sage that night. Why was Sage lying?

But then Sage looked up, gave her a quick, professional smile, and said in Russian, "Shall we begin?"

Callie dismissed her curiosity with relief in the knowledge that today it would be strictly business between her and Sage. She did not even allow herself to feel a shaft of womanly disappointment or to wonder what had brought on his change of attitude. She merely sat down, opened her books, and for the next two hours applied herself diligently to the Russian language.

Sage's office was small and cluttered, and the only place for Callie to sit was on the narrow sofa that was flanked on either side by leaning bookshelves that were crammed with dusty texts and ragged stacks of paper. It was windowless and impersonal, more like a storage place for leftover ideas than a working man's retreat. Callie could not imagine Sage spending much time here, and she was certain that the hours he did work here were an obligatory duty from which he could not wait to escape. Sage would never be comfortable in a room without windows. She wondered why he had not suggested they work outside today.

His restlessness was evident from the moment they began. Just as he did in the classroom, Sage paced as he talked, and when he gave Callie an assignment that required her silent concentration, he did not use the time to study his own papers or go over tomorrow's lesson. He perched for a moment on the desk, looked absently around the room, walked from the closed door to the opposite wall, paused to flip through a book, replaced it, and began pacing again. Another person might have been distracted or annoyed by his constant movement, but Callie found it comforting. To her, his mere presence was comforting.

After a time he sat beside her on the sofa to follow her progress in the text, pointing out her errors and showing her shortcuts. As Callie had known from the first, Sage was an excellent teacher. He made learning an effortless experience, and she was glad he had applied himself to the task at hand today. A ray of hope penetrated the despair that had previously clouded the foreign language, and she began to believe she might have a chance after all.

So intense was she upon the work before her that some time had passed in silence before Callie noticed that Sage had not resumed his restless motion. He merely sat beside her on the sofa, doing nothing at all but looking at her. She glanced guiltily at her watch. "Oh—is my time up?"

"Sure is," he replied, without much concern. One elbow was propped up against the back on the sofa and he rested his cheek on his splayed hand. He simply watched her, thoughtfully, quietly, as though he took very great pleasure in doing so. His eyes were shady and relaxed, his expression easy, his mouth resting upon the curve of what might have been a very faint smile. Why did the way he was looking at her suddenly make Callie very nervous?

She started to gather up her books. "Sorry—I guess I got carried away. This was great. I've learned so much—I think I'm getting the hang of it now." She was chattering. During the course of the afternoon, Callie had slipped her shoes off and curled her stockinged legs beneath her on the sofa. Now as she bent to retrieve her shoes, the books started to slip from her lap and Sage rescued them. But instead of returning them to her, he took them and placed them on the floor on the other side of the sofa. Then he reached out and took the one shoe she had found from her hand, placing it alongside the books.

Callie laughed a little nervously. "What are you doing?" But already she saw it in his eyes, and already her heart was beginning to speed in response to it. The professor had done his duty and had been dismissed, and now there was only the man. And the man had eyes that could strip her senseless when they smiled.

"I'm just wondering," he answered her easily, "whether I'll get to make love to you today."

Her breath caught and the sofa squeaked as he moved to take her in his arms. A brilliant awareness engulfed her and held her frozen in time, lips parted, eyes wide with anticipation, cells opening to tingling capillary action... And her chest was tight, her stomach muscles clenched, dread and anticipation, wonder and protest. For a moment Sage simply held her face cupped in his hands and smiled down at her. Callie's whole world seemed to be encompassed by his smile.

But her hands found his arms and tightened upon them; she knew she could not allow this to happen. Not again. She whispered, "Sage...don't..." And his face came down and his tongue lightly flickered over her lips.

It was playful, it was provocative, it was gentle and it was maddening. Callie was lost from that first second. His tongue darted lightly in and out, touching her teeth, brushing the inner flesh of her lips, tracing the outline from full center to corner, and the motion was like a series of jolts from a bare live wire. Heat fanned and muscles loosened and her breath floated far away on a thin stream of fading consciousness. Their mouths never met, but the expert manipulations of his tongue were more arousing than any full-bodied kiss could have been. Promising and retreating...then his thumbs pressed gently against the corners of her lips, loosening whatever resistance might have remained, and his tongue deliberately and purposefully penetrated the barrier of her mouth, slowly entering, slowly withdrawing, an intense and meaningful erotic motion that made Callie gasp out loud.

"Sage...stop." She turned her head weakly. She was barely whispering. She could hear her heart thundering. "That's—not fair."

Now his tongue swept graciously over the plane of her face, his skin hot and coarse against hers; now the warm moist probing found the sensitive hollow behind her ear and a hot shiver of pleasure exploded all the way down to her toes. "How so?" he murmured. His voice vibrated in every nerve of her body, swirling in her head, blocking out everything else.

"Sage..." It was little more than a moan.

He stopped. He looked down at her, still holding her face in his hands. The light in his eyes was brilliant and erratic, jumping and sparking like a sputtering candle. His smile was not quite playful and not quite serious, but lingering in the delight of the region somewhere in between. "It gets better," he promised.

Callie increased the pressure of her fingers on his arms, as she tried to straighten her spine. "Please," she said a little shakily. "Let me go."

"Why?" Still half-teasing. "Aren't you having fun?"

It was hard to smile, and it was hard not to. She moved his hands deliberately from her face and sat up straighter. "Just a little course in conscious relaxation after a hard session at the books, huh?" she accused him wryly.

"Never hurts." The smile lingered in his eyes, and his hands, as soon as she released them, settled on her waist. "Also, just a gentle hint that I'm really quite a good lover. I'm sure you won't be disappointed."

She laughed in pure astonishment. "You're outrageous!"

And she watched as his snapping eyes shared her mirth, then slowly settled and faded into something much gentler, much deeper. One finger lightly touched the corner of her upturned lips and lingered there before returning to embrace her waist again. "That's better," he said softly. His eyes moved over her face, caressing, appreciating, at last smiling tenderly into hers. "You do take yourself too seriously sometimes."

And her own expression faded into rueful gratitude. "There's not much chance of that as long as you're around."

But the playfulness had disappeared from his face. "Then I hope," he said quietly, "that you'll let me be around a lot." His arms slipped around her waist, pulling her to him; he kissed her.

Callie couldn't help it. Her own arms reached upward and encircled his neck, her fingers explored the warm patch of neck between hair and collar, her lips parted to welcome his entry. His curls were soft and furry to her touch, his muscles strong and sheltering as they enfolded her. The heat of his body melted into hers, leanness and hardness against softness and pliancy, and she let the dizziness come and carry her away. It was good, so good, to be held by this man, to be kissed by him...Sage, who could make her laugh at herself. Sage, who understood even when she did not. Her guide and her protector... How had she grown so close to him in such a short time? How could he mean so much to her when she did not even know him? How could they be so good together...

As Sage lifted his face slightly, his breath tickled her face, and his lips were so close they almost brushed hers as he whispered, "Did you really think I would forget wanting you in just two days?" His lips touched hers again, gently clasping and releasing and clasping again. His hand swept downward over the curve of her hip and brushed her thigh.

Callie caught his hand and turned her face. The pounding of her heart now felt like a prelude to panic. What was she doing? And why was she so afraid of what felt so right?

"I think," she said, somewhat unsteadily, "that it might be best—if you did forget it." And she turned away.

For a moment Sage's eyes were hooded and his breathing, so soft, was as irregular as Callie's. Then In a smooth and unexpected movement, he turned on the sofa, arranging his legs on either side of her, drawing her into the nest he had made with her back against his chest and his chin resting lightly on her hair. His hands were looped across her abdomen, thumbs just a fraction of an inch below the curve of her breast. It was a casually intimate embrace, and Callie found it almost more disturbing than the one from which he had just released her. "Okay," he said. His voice was conversational. "I'm listening."

Callie tried to laugh, but it was an uncomfortable sound. She wiggled a little against his embrace but made no real effort to escape. "I—don't know what you mean."

"All right, I'll start you off." Still his voice was easy and relaxed. His breath fluttered the hair across her forehead. "First, you object to making love on the sofa in a dingy office where anyone might walk in at any time—"

Now her laugh sounded more natural. "Good point."

"The door is locked," he countered. "And also, I have more taste than that myself. Secondly, you might like to tell me about all the follies and pitfalls of a teacher having an affair with his student . . ."

"Another good point." Callie was starting to relax. As long as he kept it light, as long as he stayed away from the real reasons. . .

"Wrong," he corrected implacably. "That excuse is so shallow I won't even waste time defending it. Maybe. . ." His hand came up, his fingers gently captured a strand of her bangs and curled it away from her eyes. "Maybe you'd like to tell me that you really find me repulsive, and everything I do turns you off, and you'd sooner take your pick from any man on death row than spend another minute with me."

It was a light remark, but something about his tone, or perhaps it was the feel of his fingers absently playing with her hair, caused a tightening of Callie's throat. The little laugh she forced this time bore no resemblance at all to a sound of mirth. "You're fishing for compliments."

"I'm entitled," he returned mildly. His fingers released her bangs and threaded through the hair at her temples, lifting it and letting it fall against her face, again in a sweet and sensuous motion that started a tingling in Callie's scalp and awoke the nerve endings in her fingertips.

"All right." Her voice was strained toward lightness. "I find you repulsive, and everything you do turns me off, and I'd really rather be locked in a cage with every man on death row than spend another minute with you."

"I don't believe you." He lifted her hair and placed a long, warm kiss on the nape of her neck. Callie's swiftly indrawn breath was only a reflection of the melting of muscles and the lapping heat that spread through her from the touch of his lips.

"Don't," she whispered, and arched her neck away from him.

Sage sat back, his sigh fluttering across the moisture that lingered from his lips and causing Callie to shiver. She, in turn, sat forward, drawing her knees up to her chin and looping her arms around them, her full-circle skirt hiding her legs and protecting her ankles. Callie knew the time had come for a confrontation with the truth, but she was not certain she knew what the truth was.

"You know, Callie," Sage said thoughtfully after a time, "people are funny. You can wander around your whole life without ever meeting anyone special, but then if by accident you do stumble across someone and there's the potential for something important there—the first instinct is to run. I wonder why that is?"

Callie did not answer. She only hugged her knees more tightly and turned her cheek to rest upon them so that her hair hid her face.

"I used to be that way," Sage went on in that quiet, contemplative tone. His fingers began to lightly, absently, stroke her back. "But I don't know...maybe it's getting old, maybe it's just growing up, maybe it's the kind of life I lead that makes me realize how little time there is and how much of it I've wasted on things that aren't really important. I mean..." And now his voice took on a heavy deeply reflective, almost wondering, tone, "do you realize that if I were to die today no one would really care? There's no one close enough to me to care or miss me for very long...and that's sad.''

Callie felt the tightening in her chest that was half protest, half dreadful understanding. For she knew those very words could be applied to her life as well, and it was sad. *But I would care, Sage*, she thought a little desperately. *I would miss you and what we might have had*... but she did not say the words out loud.

''So anyway...'' It was with an audible effort that he lightened his tone. Callie wished she could see his face, and then was glad she could not. Had he known that it would be easier to have this conversation if she were not looking at him? ''A couple of years ago I came to the realization that avoiding relationships was not only stupid but self-destructive, and I made up my mind to get my priorities straight. Only, lo and behold, not a single person walked through my life who held even the faintest hint of interest for me...until you.'' His wandering fingers had found the band of her bra beneath the sweater and were now tracing its outline absently, over and over in a caressing back-and-forth motion. He could have had no idea what that was doing to her. ''So tell me, Callie,'' he demanded gently. ''Tell me your very excellent reasons why we should walk away from each other when we both know there might be something special here.''

She couldn't take it any more, the intimate caresses of his fingers on her back, the gently pointed truths...how had this happened? How had they gone from barely speaking to each other to playfulness to passion to this, possibly the most serious conversation Callie had ever had with anyone in her life, in such a short time? Why was she letting him get to her?

Callie straightened her back, deliberately moving away from his touch, and she gave her head a toss. She tried with all her might to get the mood back onto a more sensible level. But she still could not turn and look at him. "Sage," she said carefully, "don't you think this might be a case of much ado about nothing? I mean, we hardly know each other after all. . ."

"That's not my fault," Sage said quietly. The movement he made to sit more conventionally on the sofa startled Callie, and so did the expression on his face when she looked at him. The playfulness was gone. There was frustration, impatience, insistence. . . all emotions she had never expected to see portrayed on that enigmatic countenance.

"Damn it, Callie," he said shortly, "you've been coming on to me and backing away from me since the first day we met—and it doesn't matter how long ago that was, the results are the same." And as she opened her mouth in protest, he continued, "I'm not talking about sex right now—that would be easy if I wanted it, and you know it." She shut her mouth abruptly, a dull color staining her cheeks, because she did know it. All he had to do was touch her and she melted. Had he only once pressed past her point of token resistance, they would have been lovers. . . and then where would

Callie's life have been? Didn't he see that she had no time for emotions right now, that she couldn't afford another person in her life...

His tone gentled as he saw the admission in her face. "No, you're cheating us both out of something more important than a physical relationship," he told her. "I meant what I said the other night. I want to be your friend. I could care for you, Callie—a lot. But every time I try to get close, you slam the door, and the worst part about that is I can see in your eyes that you don't want to. You need someone to confide in, but you won't let it be me. You refuse to give us a chance to know each other. Why?"

Callie stood, a stiff breath escaping her parted lips, and she unconsciously ran her damp palms over her wool-clad hips as she moved away from the sofa. Maybe that was the one characteristic about Sage that made Callie so uneasy. He had a way of effortlessly and unpretentiously going straight to the truth, no quarter given, no apologies offered. It was next to impossible to keep a secret from him. "Maybe," she said lowly, not looking at him, "maybe—you wouldn't like me so much if you knew me."

There was a brief silence. "I don't have the right to make that decision on my own?"

Callie shook her head, quickly and determinedly. Every muscle in her body was knotted.

She heard his breath and the rustling of sofa springs as he got up. She only tensed more as she heard him cross the room toward her. Her shoulders were like rocks as he cupped them gently with his hands. "We all have things in our lives we're ashamed of, Callie," he said very quietly. "Demons that keep us on the run. . . And sometimes we need a friend to get us through."

Callie turned slowly, questioningly, to face him. And there was something in the depths of his navy eyes that made her ask, almost in a whisper, "Do you?"

She saw the struggle that kept his customary shield of impenetrability from descending. His instinct was to deny it. It cost him not to. "Yes," he admitted quietly. "I do."

Callie knew it wasn't fair, but she had to ask him. He accused her of closing him off, but in truth Sage knew far more about Callie than she did about him. And she couldn't help it, she wanted to know him. . .as badly as he wanted to know her. "What—kind of demons?" she asked softly.

Once again she saw him fight with evasion. He could have lied to her then and she would not have known the difference. It was perhaps that acknowledgment, shared equally by both of them, that refused to allow him to do so. And half a truth was better than none. "Things from my past," he admitted quietly, and he could not quite meet her eyes as he said it. "People I got involved with when I was too young to know better. Things I'd like to forget and. . .commitments I guess I'll never escape." The last was said heavily, on the breath of a sigh that faded out his words and made them almost unintelligible. He turned away from her, as though realizing he had said too much and wondering now if it was worth the cost.

Callie's heart had begun to beat slowly and tightly during the length of his speech; a dread was forming in her stomach she could not explain. So Sage had his secrets, too. And she suddenly felt quite clearly that she did not want to know what they were.

But she found herself inquiring, with a great effort, "Commitments—to a woman?"

His smile was twisted and bitter, the sound of denial he made was harsh. "I wish. Unfortunately those kind of commitments are a lot easier to get out of than..." And he broke off abruptly, knowing he was about to go too far. A brief shake of his head finalized his resolution, and he shoved his hands in his pockets. When he turned, a small smile disguised all other emotion on his face. "Congratulations," he said. "You're very good at turning the tables. I've never met anyone who could do that to me before."

She looked at him, searching eyes that had grown dark and implacable, probing for the chink in his armor that once had been there but now had sealed itself up completely. She felt disappointed, confused, and a little hurt. "I'm sorry," she said quietly. "I didn't mean to make you uncomfortable. I have no more right to pry into your life than you have into mine."

His expression was grave, his tone sober. "So that's it, then?"

Callie turned and went back to the sofa, bending

to pick up her shoes. She wished it could be different. She wished it so badly that it hurt.

"I think," she said, slipping on her shoes and not looking at him, "that it will probably be best if we—just keep it student and teacher. There's no point in pretending it can go further."

He watched her in silence as she gathered up her books. And then, when she was at the door, he said abruptly, "I disagree. I'll see you Tuesday, Callie."

Sage stood there staring at the door for a long time after she had gone. Then he walked over to his desk, picked up the telephone, and punched out the number that would connect him with George Axom.

"I just had a conversation you need to know about," Sage told the man on the other end. His voice was cold, his face hard. His eyes never left the door where Callie had been. "Where can we meet?"

Chapter Eight

Callie's apartment no longer bore any resemblance to the type of sterile boxlike environment in which she had spent most of her life. Colorful posters plastered the walls and dubious objets d'art occupied every corner. Tandy had spread a hooked rug made out of scraps of what appeared to be last year's wardrobe square in the middle of the shag carpet, and in the center of the rug reposed a cocktail table whose base was unmistakably an elephant's foot. There was a vase of ostrich feathers on top of the table and a pile of magazines falling off it. Shadow boxes and record album racks were scattered everywhere; paperback novels and video cassettes peeked out from behind sofa cushions and tumbled off a clutter of occasional tables that were arranged in the most unlikely places. A macrame hanger suspended an empty goldfish bowl from the ceiling. For the first time in her life, Callie's apartment actually looked like a home.

And for the first time in her life, Callie could not find anything.

It was seven forty-five on Saturday evening, and Brad was due at eight. Putting aside the fact that Callie was not looking forward to the party at all, that they were presently in the midst of a cold and furious rainstorm, and that she could think of nothing she wanted to do more than curl up in bed with a good book—forgetting the fact that she was three chapters behind in World Economics and she had two days to prepare a paper that would take her a week to write—Callie could not find the suede vest she had purchased only last week and she had already spent too much time trying to piece together an outfit for this party to start over now.

She heard the front door slam and she relaxed her frantic search with a sigh. "Tandy!" Her expression was formidable as she came through the door into the living room. "Have you seen my new vest?"

Tandy was dripping puddles onto the carpet by the front door, pushing back the hood of her garish lavender slicker and wiping raindrops off her glasses with a soggy newspaper ad. "It's a mess out there!" She replaced her glasses and squinted at Callie through the smeared lenses. "Are you going out? I don't envy you!"

"Not," Callie said pointedly, "unless I can find my vest. You're dripping all over the rug!"

"Oh..." Tandy absently waved the stack of water-logged mail she had collected. "You loaned it to me last week, remember? It's on my bed somewhere. Hey..." She peered at one of the envelopes. "Here's a letter for you."

Callie retrieved it, scowling. She did not recall loaning the vest to Tandy, but she knew better than to make a point of it. Arguing with her scatter-brained roommate was nothing but a waste of breath.

She glanced at the letter as she turned toward Tandy's room, and then stopped. It had been forwarded from her old address, and she recognized the handwriting with a leap of excitement. Quickly she tore open the soggy envelope. Maybe he had something for her. . .

Tried tracing you through the university, but the dorms had no record of you. . . Guess you changed your mind about that hare-brained scheme. I hope so. How about calling a fellow sometime? Are you still in the States? Are you still alive? I've got better things to do than track you down, you know. Nothing to say— just want to check in.

Love,
Jerry

Callie folded the letter with a regretful smile that was half nostalgia, half guilt. He was right, of course. She should have called him. She had only been avoiding it because of the lecture he was sure to give her. . .

"Damn!" The low, fierce exclamation behind her caused Callie to turn in surprise. She had never heard her roommate swear before, and neither had she seen that tight look of anger, the white lips, the streaks of scarlet temper that crept from Tandy's temple to cheeks. Tandy crumpled the letter she was reading stiffly in her fist and hissed again, furiously, *"Damn!"*

Such raw emotion on the usually moonlike face was shocking, to say the least. Callie took an alarmed step toward her friend. "Tandy—what is it? What's wrong?"

Tandy's eyes shot at Callie as though she had forgotten her presence. They were glittering with repressed emotion, and for a moment Callie almost didn't recognize the mild-mannered, other-worldly person with whom she had shared her home for almost a month. Then Tandy whirled abruptly, marched over to the trash can, and began to shred the letter into fine pieces. It was awhile before she could speak.

"It's my father," Tandy choked out at last, watching the last of the pieces flutter into the trash can. She glared at it for a moment, then gave the trash can a furious kick. It echoed with a metallic clang through the tension that snapped in the room. *"Damn* it all!" she cried. "Why can't he leave me alone?"

Callie took a hesitant step toward Tandy. "Tandy, I don't understand. . .what's he done? Why—"

"He's coming here, that's what he's done!" Tandy cried viciously, and then forcefully regained her temper. She shoved her fists into the crinkly pockets of her raincoat and took a breath, a look of reluctant apology crossing her face. "Sorry," she muttered. "I shouldn't take it out on you." And she turned away, her small head bowed, her shoulders tense and hunched beneath the shiny lavender fabric.

Callie was torn. She was late and her friend needed her. This was a side of Tandy she had never seen and it confused and disturbed Callie, but even more confusing was Tandy's reaction to the simple news that her father was paying a visit. Callie did not understand. She did not know what to say.

"Lord," said Tandy at last, lowly, "looks like for once in his life—just once—he could leave me alone. I came two thousand miles to get away from him, and even that wasn't far enough!" She laughed, shortly and dryly. "What do I have to do? I mean, what the hell do I have to *do*?"

Callie could not relate to her friend's distress at all. She knew that some families did not get along; she knew she should not sit in judgment upon anyone, but she thought about how she had come two thousand miles to find her father and the entire situation struck her as terribly ironic. And all Callie really wanted to tell Tandy was how lucky she was, how Callie would have given the world and all that was in it to have opened a letter that said her father was coming to visit. . . It was hard to keep her tone kind, but Callie tried. "Tandy," she offered, "don't you think you're making a big deal out of nothing? I mean, everyone's parents come to visit every once in a while. Naturally he's interested in seeing how you're getting along. . .it's not as though he's moving in or anything. . ."

Again Tandy laughed, but it sounded more as

though she were on the verge of tears. "*Me*, make a big deal? You haven't met my father yet! You talk about big deals!"

The doorbell rang then, and Callie did not know whether to be relieved or annoyed. She glanced at her roommate, and Tandy sniffled, turned, and squared her shoulders. The grimace she made was an effort at a smile. "Go on, get ready for your date," she said. "Sorry I blew up on you. I'll get the door."

Callie hesitated, more out of politeness than real concern. Actually she thought Brad's timing could not have been more perfect. Another moment and she would have been forced to tell Tandy exactly what she thought of her spoiled-brat attitude, for her sympathy with her roommate's problem was fading fast. It was an old case of the have's and the have-not's, and Callie's jealousy was showing. She was ashamed of herself, but she couldn't help it. Tandy did not know how lucky she was.

Callie called hello to Brad as Tandy opened the door, told him she was almost ready, and then rushed off in search of her vest. This was not starting out to be much of a night.

Callie did not know much about what young people were wearing to parties these days—in fact, she did not know much about young people's parties at all—but she thought her tan corduroys, white turtleneck, and Tandy's knee-length boots would do. The vest, of course, was the finishing touch. Callie looked comfortable but not too underdressed, stylish but not trendy. She had pinned back one side of her hair with a ribbonned barrette that sported a single pale brown feather—again borrowed from Tandy's collection—and had to reluctantly admit that, considering half her wardrobe had come from Tandy's closet, she could not afford to be too angry about the vest incident. She also resolved to have a nice long chat with her roommate when she got home after the party and to be the very essence of charity when it came to pretending to sympathize with Tandy's parental difficulties.

But by the time Callie came out, Brad seemed to have all but taken care of that problem for her. Callie could hardly believe that this was the same girl who had had murder in her eyes five minutes ago. Her cheeks were glowing a subtle pink that clashed raucously with the lavender coat, her eyes were sparkling, she was laughing softly as she talked to Brad and was using every womanly signal in the book to telegraph the fact that she had just been swept off her feet by a knight in shining armor. And Callie did not have to be a person of unusual perception to observe that the attraction was mutual. Amused, she wished she could think of some way to send Tandy to the party in her place, thus pleasing everyone involved, but such things only worked out gracefully in situation comedies. Maybe next time.

Callie got her purse and her coat and was standing at the door before Brad even looked up. When she interrupted the conversation to ask if he was ready, there was real reluctance in his face as he got to his feet and joined her. The smile that lingered in his eyes was for Tandy alone, and he hardly glanced at Callie.

In the hallway he commented casually, "Nice girl."

Callie did not bother to suppress a grin. "Yeah. Too bad you didn't meet her before you asked me out."

Brad's grin was sheepish, embarrassed, and a little reluctant, "Then you wouldn't mind if I—uh—asked her out sometime?"

Callie laughed. "Be my guest! As a matter of fact, you can leave me here and take Tandy to the party, if you like!"

"I'm too much of a gentleman for that!" he protested, but his eyes were sparkling and he impulsively flung an arm around Callie's shoulders and squeezed her tightly. "You're a great girl, you know that? And," he added, sobering a little, "just for that, I want you to know I'm not going to hang all over you tonight. I mean, just because you came with me doesn't mean you have to leave with me, you know? No hard feelings. We're friends."

Callie laughed a little and shook her head helplessly. She had no choice but to agree to his very generous terms.

The rain had slowed somewhat, but still Callie's conservative London Fog raincoat was soaked by the time they reached the curb where Brad's Trans Am was parked. "Nice car," Callie commented as Brad opened the door for her. "Did your folks give it to you?"

"What! Are you kidding?" Brad scoffed. "They

won't even give me the time of day until my grades improve. Nope," he informed her smugly, "I worked for this baby, just like I did for my computer system."

Callie lifted an appreciative eyebrow. So the younger generation had more character than she had thought. Or maybe Brad was just an exception to the rule.

Brad started the engine and turned on the heater, but before pulling away from the curb, he reached across Callie to take something from the map compartment. "I just got this in today," he said. "Sorry it took so long, but I'd never run this program before."

Callie's heart stopped, then lurched into an excited, shallow rhythm as Brad handed her a folded computer printout. She had been afraid to ask him about it before, afraid of being disappointed, afraid he couldn't do it, wanting to hope for as long as possible. . . She managed in an almost normal tone, "Any troubles?"

"Nah." He switched on the interior lamp as she unfolded the papers with unsteady hands. "Just time-consuming. Hope it helps your friend."

"I—I'm sure it will. . .thanks so much. . ." Callie scanned three pages of computer information about two men who were dead and in whom she had no interest whatsoever. Then she came to the last page, "Frye, Jedidah. . ." And the words blinked incredulously before her eyes, "Code 47. . . Code 47. . . Code 47. . ."

"I—don't understand," she said weakly. Her

disappointment was so acute it tasted like bile in her throat. This couldn't be. Her last hope, her closest chance. . .it couldn't be.

Brad leaned over her, frowning a little in agreement. "I know," he said. "It's the freakiest thing. I tried everything I knew to break past the code, but no dice. Somebody sure has it rigged." There was both resentment and amazement in his voice. Obviously Brad was more than a little offended that someone had interfered with his system. . .and adding insult to injury, that someone knew more about his computer than he did.

Callie stared at the paper for a long time, her head whirling. Why should she be so surprised? She knew it was a long shot. If there was information to be obtained, Jerry would have gotten it long before now. What made her think she could just break into an FBI file and solve the whole problem with the push of a button? It served her right, anyway. What she had done was illegal and this was poetic justice. Besides, if the FBI knew the whereabouts of Jed Frye, they would have been down upon him before now, so the entire point was moot. It had been a stupid idea.

And none of that explained why the file had been deleted. There were complete dossiers on the other two men she had listed. But, of course, they were dead. Then why. . .?

Something indefinable and queasy was forming in the pit of her stomach. She said slowly, "Brad. . . isn't this the same code the computer gave us when we asked for the file on Sage McCormick?"

Brad nodded. In the yellow overhead light his face was grim. "That's what was so crazy about it," he agreed. "I mean, I couldn't figure it out. So I ran Code Forty-seven through the whole system and sure enough—the only two files it showed on were McCormick's and Frye's. Weird, huh?"

Callie was totally out of her depth. She knew this meant something, but she was too uneducated in the intricacies of computers to imagine what it was... or perhaps she was just too afraid. "I don't understand," she said again, very weakly, and she half hoped Brad would not enlighten her.

"It means," Brad informed her carefully, "that whoever wiped out McCormick's file also wiped out Frye's... and that whoever did it was either very smart or very powerful. I mean, we're talking about a code that blocks out access all the way to the FBI. That's not exactly kid's stuff, you know."

Callie stared at him. She felt as though her brain were a victim of jet lag, just a few steps behind the rest of the world. Eventually she would figure it out, eventually she would understand what Brad was obviously trying to tell her, but right now it was just a little bit beyond her reach.

"It also means," Brad said, his face still very guarded and his tone precise and clear, "that whoever did it—whoever is responsible—is operating from within the university system, right here on campus."

Callie was dazed. Echoing over in her brain were Jerry's words, "There's evidence to indicate that Jed Frye might be on campus. . ." Was this it then?

Was this the proof she needed? But *what* proof? It made no sense. "But—who could it be?" she queried. "Who would want to. . . I mean, why?"

Brad looked at her very soberly. "I don't know, Callie," he said. "The only connection I can think of between Jed Frye and Sage McCormick is you."

Callie's eyes widened; her head reeled. But this, at least, she could understand. "Brad—you can't possibly think that I—!"

His expression remained carefully neutral. "It does seem like pretty much of a coincidence, don't you think," he said "that the only two files you asked for were also the only two files that came up Code Forty-seven?"

For a moment Callie was speechless. Of what was he accusing her? Yet it was a coincidence, almost too much of a coincidence to be believed, and there was something there, something she was overlooking. . . "But—but," she sputtered, "why would I— I don't even know how to work a computer! And why. . ."

Brad's long and probing look gradually faded and he shook his head slightly. "That's the one thing I couldn't figure out. You could be lying about your computer experience, of course, but it didn't make sense that you would ask me to retrieve files you'd already deleted. But if you didn't do it," he put to her pointedly, "who did?"

Callie's heart was pounding to the regular, hypnotic sound of rain against the windshield. Somehow this thing had been turned around so that she was being accused of who-knew-what, and Callie was not used to defending herself against unknown crimes. And the worst was that Brad's suspicions were only logical. . . she was the only connection between Sage and Jed Frye.

It was there that her heart gave a magnificent thump that almost made her gasp out loud. Sage McCormick. Jed Frye. A connection. Someone, or something, besides Callie that they had in common. . . what could it be? What could it possibly be? In what way could Sage McCormick be involved with an underground terrorist who had been in hiding for the past fifteen years?

Brad's long, heavy breath penetrated the foggy racing of Callie's mind. His expression was very grave, his voice quiet. "Look, Callie," he said. "I don't really think you programmed that code into the computer. It just doesn't make sense for one thing, and for another. . ." He tried to smile. "I guess I really want to believe that you wouldn't play games like that with me. But. . ." And now his face grew sober again, "if whatever you're involved in has something to do with Sage McCormick, I wish you'd tell me."

Callie simply stared at him.

Brad must have misinterpreted the confusion and incredulity on her face as stubbornness, for he sighed in acknowledgment and touched her hair in a brief, friendly gesture. "Okay," he said softly. "It's your business, I guess. Just be careful, okay?"

At last she managed to speak. The dread in the pit of her stomach was making her nauseous. "What—what do you mean?"

"McCormick." He said the word curtly, and turned to the steering wheel. "Just watch your step around him. Word has it that...well, he hangs around with some pretty tough characters. He's not a man to fool around with."

But only two things were pulsing in Callie's brain as Brad put the car into gear. Someone on this campus besides Callie was interested in Jed Frye. And that interest increased the possibilities by one hundred percent that her father had been here...and perhaps still was.

Callie was in a daze as she walked with Brad through alternating drizzle and drenching downpour that accompanied their course from the car to a small house almost a block away. From the number of vehicles that lined the street, it would be quite a crowded party, and muted music greeted them as soon as they reached the driveway. Brad opened the door without knocking, and they stepped into a loud, smoky, dimly lit room crowded with bodies of every size and shape. Brad had to shout as he helped her off with her coat, but his smile was reassuring. "Remember," he said, "the point is to mingle! I'll get you something to drink."

Callie shouted back her thanks, but he did not hear her as he disappeared into the musty depths of the room.

This certainly promised to be an educational experience, but Callie felt as though she had been educated quite sufficiently for one night and only wanted to go home and try to make sense out of what she had learned from Brad. Her brain was so crowded now that one more impulse was likely to send her into the depths of a migraine—if the smoke and the noise did not do it first. She tried to relax and put everything out of her mind until she got home where she could analyze properly, but she knew that would be an almost impossible task.

There was an occasional burst of high laughter above pulsating base rhythms of rock music, there were a few couples dancing, but surprisingly enough most of the people were drawn into tight little conversational knots. There was the usual amount of home-rolled cigarettes being passed around, but none of those people gathered into groups appeared to be sharing one. They were actually talking, and that puzzled Callie. Why would people come to a party like this to engage in such serious conversations? And why would they try to do it under the cover of all this noise?

Callie did not have to be a narcotics expert to guess that the shallow bowl on a table in the center of the room that was attracting so much attention did not contain onion dip. These were all college students; some of them she even recognized from her classes. Since when could college kids afford to serve cocaine at a party this size?

Times were changing, she supposed.

There was a man in a corner with long, dark hair and a battered sombrero with the brim cut out smoking a water pipe. He had gathered a group of supplicants around him like a guru, all of them sitting crossed-legged on the floor at his feet, all of them talking quietly to him. But he was not talking.

He was staring at Callie. His face was lean and harsh, his appearance grimy, his eyes cold and calculating and seeming to bore right through Callie. An uneasy shiver rippled through her stomach muscles. Why had he singled her out? The man was obviously wasted out of his skull, but his eyes were clear and alert, just as though he knew exactly who she was and what she was doing here... And then he suddenly shifted his gaze, spoke quietly to someone just out of Callie's range of vision, and nodded in her direction. Callie turned quickly away. This whole thing was beginning to give her the creeps.

She spotted Brad across the room, deep in conversation with someone else. Annoyed that she had been deserted, but then recalling he had not made her any promises, Callie started to inch through the crowd toward him anyway. Maybe she could persuade him to leave for just a few minutes and take her home. This was definitely not her kind of party.

Her arm was grabbed from behind, and it was evidence of Callie's tightly strung nerves that she actually gasped out loud and whirled, ready to fight. The young man quickly released her and held up his hands, grinning, in a sign of peace. But that did not relax Callie any. The man she was facing had a droopy mustache and a curly hairdo. It was the same person she had seen in Sage's office the other day, the one who had confronted Sage in the shadows of a misty street on their first evening together... the man Sage denied knowing.

"Hi," he said. "You're Callie, right?"

Callie tried not to let her nervousness show. He

seemed harmless enough, but there was something about him she didn't like...maybe it was his eyes. She couldn't help remembering the way they had stripped her that day he was leaving Sage's office. "Do I know you?" she asked.

"You've probably seen me around," he admitted. "I audit your Mideastern affairs class sometimes." And his smile reminded Callie of a rubber mask; it made her feel cold. "I'm glad you came."

Callie tried to dismiss the unreasonable repulsion she felt for him. He was a friend of Sage's, wasn't he? He couldn't be all bad... "Oh," she said, forcing friendliness into her tone. "Is this your party? I came with someone and—"

"Yeah, I know," he interrupted. "Brad. He did a good job, getting you here. A lot of people here want to meet you."

Callie frowned a little, puzzled. "Meet me? Why?"

His cold, dark eyes twinkled as though they shared a private joke. "Oh. I think you'll find we all have a lot in common. You're a friend of Brad's, aren't you? And McCormick? A girl with your background...I'm sure you'd have a lot to add to our little Tuesday-night study groups."

A smooth, familiar voice said behind her, "Good evening, Callie."

Callie turned. Sage's face was so cold and his eyes so hard that it shocked her. The smile of relieved greeting died on her lips as he took her arm. "Would you like to dance?" he asked, still in that pleasantly casual tone, but Callie could feel anger radiating through his fingers, coursing through every muscle of his body, and she had a feeling that if she refused he would forcibly drag her away.

The young man smiled and said, "See you around, Callie," as Sage took her in his arms.

Callie rested her hands against Sage's shoulders and looked up at him, her confusion showing in her face. He rested his hands on her waist but did not pull her close. His body was stiff and he made only the most cursory effort to move with the rhythm of the music. His face was completely implacable, and he said lowly, "What are you doing here?"

He did not look at her as he spoke, and Callie thought it was just as well. She was almost afraid of what she would see in his eyes. Why was he so angry? "I came with a friend," she said, trying to keep it pleasant. "I didn't have any idea you were going to be here."

"Then I guess we both had a little surprise tonight." He made a sudden turn to avoid a couple who had had a little too much of whatever it was that made them happy, and their thighs brushed. He immediately moved to put distance between them again.

Callie did not know what to say. This seemed to be her day for seeing sides of people she had never imagined. First Tandy, now Sage. . . What had gotten into him? She made one more attempt to keep the conversation civil. "How did you find me? I didn't see you when I came in."

"A friend pointed you out."

Callie followed the direction of his nod and then

her eyes flew back to him in surprise. "The creep with the water pipe?"

Sage's smile was vague and did not shadow his eyes. "Axom," he told her. "A creep, but not as bad as some."

Callie looked up at him in confusion. "But—how did he know me?" For that matter, how had the little fellow in the droopy mustache known her? Why did she feel suddenly as though she were living in a fishbowl?

"A lot of people here know you," Sage returned casually. "Or would like to." A slow-moving chill went through Callie as she recalled that those very same words had been said to her before, not five minutes ago. She did not like this. Not at all. "After all," Sage continued easily, "with your background and interests, you could be quite an asset."

Callie had had enough. Enough confusion, enough hints and innuendos, enough accusations and suspicion. She dropped her hands from Sage's shoulder and stood still. "What," she demanded, quietly and distinctly, "are you talking about?"

And nothing changed on Sage's face, nothing penetrated the steel barrier of cool hostility he had erected between them. "Come on, Callie," he said harshly. "In the past five years you've been in every hot spot in the world. Coups and revolutions, economic collapse and governmental corruption—you've been on the inside while it all was happening. You have a fluency in Russian and enough Arabic to start a nice-sized war, and you won't tell anyone how you got it. You knew exactly where to go when you came back to this country. The only courses you're taking are the ones that are designed to put you right in the center of the action and . . ." He broke off with a breath. "Damn you," he said. His voice was low and expressionles. If anything, there might have been a hint of conversational pleasantry in his tone. "You almost had me convinced."

His hands still rested on her waist and Callie could feel the tension snapping through them. Anyone observing them would have thought they were nothing more than two lovers engaged in conversation, and it occurred to Callie suddenly that that was the way Sage wanted it. She tried to step away, but his fingers tightened, pinching into the flesh of her waist. She felt her throat begin to close around the beating of her heart. "Let me go, Sage," she said hoarsely.

For just a second something very close to uncertainty flickered in his eyes. His fingers lightened imperceptibly, and Callie could have escaped then if she had wanted to. But something made her stay. It was something that was knotting in her chest and felt like tears; it could have been hurt or it could have been fear. She had to know. "Why are you so angry with me?" she whispered.

"I told you," he said simply, his eyes growing blank again, "I don't like secrets. Maybe I didn't tell you I like lies even less."

Lies. She had never lied to him. What was he talking about? Why did the fact that she had worked overseas upset him? What difference did it make where she had learned to speak Russian and why did he care what courses she took? Her head was aching and she thought it might have been due to backed-up tears. She stepped away from him.

"I learned Russian," she told him with quiet dignity, "from a cab driver. Where did you learn it?"

And she turned and made her way through the crowd, looking for her coat.

Callie did not know how she was going to find her way home. Brad was nowhere to be found, and suddenly she did not want to linger in that room a moment longer than necessary. She found her coat on a chair by the door and slipped out into the night.

A cold drizzle was still shrouding the streets and Callie tightened the belt of her raincoat, turning up the collar. The spooky red glow of changing weather conditions overshadowed the low, gray sky, a storm warning that blended night into day. She started quickly down the drive, shoving her hands into her pockets and bending her head, moving away from the suddenly sinister atmosphere of the little house as though its corruption were a tangible thing that could reach out tendrillike fingers to grab her.

There was a hollow atmosphere to the night that echoed her footsteps and sent back her own shadow to chase her. The scuttle of wet leaves sounded like little animals at her heels, and the drip of rain could have been whispers. Mist-shrouded streetlights threw skeletal branches into stark relief, and they waved like ghostly arms overhead. The cold air hurt her lungs, but maybe that was only because she was walking so fast. She suddenly realized the folly of leaving the party alone, of walking through the deserted streets without a clear direction of where she was going. . . . She could have sworn she heard footsteps behind her.

Those *were* footsteps. A very definite click and scrape against the concrete, a stride longer and heavier than her own but matching hers, moving faster as she did and gaining on her. . . Callie's ears roared and her breath fanned a screen of fog before her as she increased her pace, now breaking into a run, and the footsteps were louder, closer, and now she could almost feel the breathing on her neck. . .

She let out a cry as a hand grabbed her arm and whirled her roughly around. Her knees sagged and all the breath left her body as she saw it was Sage.

"Come on," he said shortly. "I'll drive you home."

But Callie's knees were still rubbery and she almost tripped as Sage gave her arm a little tug. She tried not to gasp for breath, but her heart was pounding so painfully she thought her ribs would crack. "Wait," she pleaded weakly. "Don't—walk so fast."

He slowed his steps and gave her a peculiar glance. "Did I scare you?"

"Only out of ten years," she managed, trying to stop shaking.

The concern she thought she saw on his face faded

into a scowl. "Serves you right," was all he said. "You should know better than to leave a party like that alone. Whom did you come with, anyway?"

But something within Callie refused to let her answer. Perhaps it was a misplaced sense of loyalty, perhaps it was simply an uneasiness caused by too much information and not enough time to digest it. She was afraid to think it might be because she did not know who to trust anymore.

Brad's voice echoed faintly in her ears, "Word has it he hangs out with some pretty rough characters..."

Callie tried not to listen.

"So," Sage murmured, and he dropped his arm. "More secrets."

Callie let the pace of her breathing be guided by his steps as they walked back up the street. The cold was a wet and invading kind; she could not stop shivering. And Sage said nothing; he merely shoved his hands into the pockets of his leather jacket and kept his eyes straight ahead, stopping at last before a red Volvo parked at the curb.

"I—thought you had a motorcycle," Callie commented as he opened the door for her. She had to make a concentrated effort to keep her teeth from chattering.

"Not practical in the winter," he answered, putting an end to desultory conversation both with his tone and with the slamming of the car door as she slid inside.

The heater did not have time to warm on the short drive back to Callie's apartment, and a cold blast of air turned her legs and booted feet to ice. She shivered and huddled against the door and Sage did not speak. She could not remember ever being so confused or miserable in her life. She had never felt so isolated and alone.

At last she could stand it no longer. Callie turned to look at him, fighting down another shiver, and she tried to keep her voice steady as she asked, "What did you mean—a party like that?"

His eyes did not leave the road, and his face was too shadowed to discern his expression. His voice was blank and disinterested. "You really don't know?"

"If you mean," she managed carefully, still trying to keep her teeth from chattering, "because of all the drugs—and things... I've been in places that would make that party look like a Sunday school picnic."

The sound Sage made was dry and harsh. "I'm sure you have."

"I'm a big girl," she said distinctly. "I know how to take care of myself. There's no reason for you—"

"Come off it, Callie," Sage interrupted roughly. His sharp tone startled her, and she could see his hands tighten on the steering wheel in the brief flash of a streetlight. "No more games, okay? We both know what that party was about, and we both know what you were doing there. There's no point in it any more."

Callie felt very strongly that the next words she said would be some of the most important ones of her life. Her mouth was actually dry, and the shivers that continuously wracked her body were from more than cold. "Then why don't you tell me," she suggested very quietly. "Tell me what it was about."

"Recruitment, damn it!" he exploded at her viciously. "Recruitment for—" And he broke off suddenly, looking at her, and something in her face seemed to confuse him. A heavy breath was all that remained of what he might have said.

Silence echoed in the car as he pulled it to the curb in front of her apartment. The motor hummed, just now beginning to put out a little heat against Callie's toes, and the windshield wipers squeaked away the clinging mist from the windows.

"Recruitment for what?" Callie said softly, and her eyes, her ears, every sense in her body strained toward him, waiting for him. . .

Sage leaned forward and turned off the windshield wipers, then the lights. Only the steady purr of the engine and the trickling sounds of rain on the roof separated them. He leaned back in the seat, looking straight ahead, and after a long time he said, tiredly, "I'm getting too old for this." And still he did not turn to her. His voice was very soft. "Why do I want to believe you so much?"

Callie should have left then. She should have gotten out of the car and walked the twenty yards to the safety of her apartment; she should have left him sitting there and forgotten about the entire ugly episode. She did not know why she lingered. Perhaps it was because she felt in imminent danger of losing something very fragile, something she had not realized was so important to her until Sage threatened to destroy it with his wall of secrecy. Bad things were happening here, things she did not want to analyze and could not accept. Perhaps she stayed because there were questions to be answered and mysteries to be unraveled that could change her whole life, and it seemed to her at that moment that Sage held the key to it all.

Sage slid down a few inches in the seat, leaning his head against the backrest, and his fingers absently played with the steering wheel. "You realize, of course," he said conversationally, "that you've put me in a very awkward position. If you're telling the truth—if you're really as innocent as you claim—anything I say to you could put you, and me, in danger. But if you're lying..." He turned his head slowly to look at her. In the false light of rain and shadows, his face looked very young, very vulnerable. "Damn it," he said softly. "Why is it so hard for me to believe you're lying?" And he turned his head to look straight ahead again. "I never asked for this," he said lowly, heavily.

Callie's hand moved on her lap, instinctively going to touch him, to smooth away those lines of worry and hurt on his face, to comfort him in whatever way she could... but her fingers curled back on themselves before the motion was completed. What did he want from her? Of what was he accusing her?

Who was he, this man with whom she was rapidly falling in love, and what dark secrets kept him away from her?

Falling in love. The phrase crept up on her like a beam of light struggling to make its way through the fog that surrounded them. Was that what was happening to her, then? Was she falling in love with this stranger...

"Callie," he said, drawing her abruptly away from a tenuous exploration of possibilities and into the uncertainty of the present. She heard the whispering sound of movement as he turned his head to look at her, and then, slowly, his hand came out and lightly closed around hers. His fingers were cold, but when her own fingers entwined with his, she thought they began to warm. His eyes were very intense in the shadows, almost black. Callie knew this was not easy for him to say. And her very soul seemed to strain toward him, trying to make it easier for him, aching to understand.

"A long time ago," Sage said quietly, "I got involved with things I never should have. Glorious principles, high ideals... all the wrong things for all the right reasons." His eyes focused away from her into the dim regions of his past, and Callie ached for him, knowing there was no way she could draw him back, wanting to follow him and knowing she could not... "I was on the border of Czechoslovakia when the Soviets invaded," Sage said, and Callie knew he was no longer speaking to her. This was his secret, long buried within the dark regions of his soul, and confession was his exoneration. "That's where I learned to speak Russian—from the natives. I lived there for three years and came to know and love the people... I thought I was doing the right thing. Causes, philosophies..." His indrawn breath was sharp and painful. It signified things done that could not be changed, history written that could not be untold, and it tore at Callie's heart. "That all meant nothing when the killing started. The things I saw, the things I did...they'll haunt me for the rest of my life." And then suddenly his eyes came back to her, dark and insistent and underscored with pain. "But that's not the worst part," Sage said. "The worst part is that even now I can't get away. Don't you see, Callie, I tried to walk away and they wouldn't let me..." His fingers tightened on hers, warm now and desperate, as though if he loosened his grip she might be lost forever. "I don't want to see the same thing happen to you."

Callie did not understand. None of it made sense. Why was he telling her this? What was he afraid of...?

But deep inside it did make sense, a horrible and deadly kind of sense. Callie just did not want to understand. Because all she felt at that moment was need for him, caring for him, wanting to make whatever was hurting him go away, wanting to hold him. She loved him. She knew that now, and nothing else at that moment mattered.

Her fingers tightened on his, and her free hand came out to lightly touch his face. She wanted to hold him, to love him, to tell him...to somehow make it better for him. "Sage..." she whispered.

Callie saw the softening of his eyes; she felt the slight movement of his face that wanted to turn into her palm. Then his hand came up and lightly captured hers, moving it away from his face but still holding it. "I don't know why I should care so much," he said quietly, "but I do. Please be careful, Callie."

The rain formed a shattered pattern of interlocking droplets on the windshield, and the light that filtered through it was yellow-gray and surrealistic. Everything was still, silent, waiting. On nights like this it was easy to be scared. On nights like this Callie wanted to be warm in someone's bed, wrapped in someone's arms, safe and secure from all that might threaten her...

The air around them was warm now, but Callie was still cold. There was an emptiness inside her, a yearning that begged to be released; a need backed up within her that knew no words for expression. She wanted to say something, to do something, to chase away the fear and the uncertainty and the nebulous threats that seemed to hang over them, but she did not know what to do. So she stayed silent.

And then, very slowly, Sage gathered her into his arms. His breath was warm and moist on her neck, and the lingering kiss he placed there penetrated her skin and melted into her muscles, encompassing all of her and blending her into him.

"Ah, Callie," he whispered, and the sorrow that was in his voice frightened her more than anything else he had said tonight. "I guess we couldn't have come into each other's lives at a worse time."

He released her, and she turned toward the door.

There was more, much more to be said, but it would
not be tonight. She could not deal with it tonight.

Sage was still parked there, watching her, as
Callie went up the drive and let herself into the
apartment. That was when she realized that from
the time Sage had stopped the car she had not said a
word.

She simply had not known what to say.

Chapter Nine

The apartment was quiet when Callie went in. It was not yet ten o'clock and Tandy was in bed. That both surprised and worried Callie. Her roommate must have been more upset than she realized, and she even allowed herself a small stab of guilt for not having been more sympathetic earlier. But all that seemed so far away now...a world had changed since the last time Callie saw Tandy.

Callie shrugged out of her coat and dropped her purse, wandering around the apartment as though the simple act of movement could take her away from the demons of the mind that chased her. Her hands were tightly clasped before her and her throat was tight. She couldn't seem to slow down the beating of her heart, and the pain that curled in her stomach was the remnants of Sage's good-bye kiss. It was too much. Too much for one night...

In a moment of decision Callie went to the telephone and dialed a long-distance number. After what seemed like forever, the connection was made, and three rings later Callie's heart was in her throat.

Why was she doing this? She did not want to do this. If she put it into words, she would have the answer, and she wasn't sure whether she could face those answers. . .

On the fourth ring the receiver clattered off the hook and a gruff voice barked, "What?"

Callie had half lowered the phone to hang up, her courage having deserted her. But at the sound of that familiar voice and the rude greeting, she almost smiled. The effort made her face hurt. "Would you believe a wrong number?" she managed, mustering a semblance of the bantering tone with which she usually greeted him.

There was a hesitance, then uncertainly, "Callie? What the hell?" He was waking up, and his displeasure in the fact was reflected in his tone. "When I said call, I didn't mean in the middle of the. . .what time is it anyway?"

"Early," she answered. "Rough day?"

"Rough week." He yawned. "Don't hang up, babe; I'm sitting here stark naked and freezing to death. Back in a minute."

Callie winced as the receiver clattered against a floor or a table on the other end, and she was starting to relax. It was good to hear Jerry's voice. If only this could be a social call, just a few minutes to chat with an old friend. . .and her muscles started to clench again as she faced the real reason for this telephone call and the fact that the ensuing moments would be far from relaxing. She should hang up. She never should have called. She did not want to hear what Jerry had to tell her and did not want to put her fears into words. . .

"Okay, I'm back." Callie heard the flick of the lighter as he lit the perpetual cigarette, heard the inhalation of nicotine that would start his blood pumping again and open his eyes. "What's up?"

She tried to imagine Jerry, competent and in control, sitting in the dark in a tattered robe, smoking a cigarette, and frowning with concentration, and the image brought a little comfort. He would know what to do. He would make sense of it all. He would tell her she was on the wrong track entirely, he would tell her she was wasting his time and hers, he would tell her all her suspicions were groundless. . . or he might not.

Callie started out slowly, telling him where she was and how she had been doing, asking about his job, talking about her studies, until he cut through her rambling with a brusque, "Save it for Old Home Week, Cal. You interrupted the first full night's sleep I've had in six days, so it had better be good. What's up?"

Callie took a breath. Better, she told herself. Better this way. Once she put it into words, she would realize that she had no proof at all, and there really was no reason to wake Jerry up in the middle of the night, no reason to be upset, no reason to hope or fear. . .

"Jed Frye," she said with a breath. "I think—he might really be here."

She could sense Jerry's attention sharpen, but his tone was noncommittal. "Go on," he invited.

Carefully, Callie told him about running Frye's name through the computer. With each word Jerry's excitement became increasingly palpable;

his silence was thick with it. "Why would anyone on campus delete that particular name?" she questioned. "Unless—unless it was Frye himself?" She was reaching, she knew she was. It sounded frail even to her own ears.

"Or unless. . ." Callie heard him exhale smoke; she could imagine him stubbing out one cigarette and fumbling for another. "Somebody knew what you were after." It took one heartbeat for him to light another cigarette. The silence was ominous and his finishing words no more comforting. "And wanted to make damn sure you didn't find it."

"But—who?" Callie said weakly. She had to sit down. Paranoia was engulfing her. Who, indeed? Tonight she had learned she was being watched by men whose names she did not even know, that she was being targeted for something, she knew not what. . .

"Are you sure it was done from within the university system?" he demanded.

Callie nodded, then remembered to speak out loud. Her voice sounded a little thready. "Y—yes. I'm sure. The person who told me—is an expert."

"Listen," he said abruptly, coming to one of his swift and usually impulsive decisions. "Do you know about the Red Knights?"

"The—what?"

Again he puffed cigarette smoke into the receiver. It was an impatient, frustrated sound. "It's an organization of political activists—hell, call a spade a spade. Terrorists. We know they're based on the university campus—used to be pretty much small-time, but lately it's starting to look like outside powers might be involved..."

"Do you mean..." Her voice was almost a whisper. "Other countries?"

People who might be found in a course on Mideastern Affairs, studying coups and revolutions in other nations...people who spoke Arabic or Russian fluently...

A distasteful little radical paper in Sage McCormick's briefcase. A Tuesday-night study group. "A girl with your background could be quite an asset..."

Callie felt sick.

"That's the way it usually goes, babe," Jerry was saying. "The thing is, these kind of things are always being watched, and when I got the scoop that Frye might also be on that campus—well, it just seemed like too much of a coincidence to ignore. I would have laid it all out for you sooner if I had had any idea you might really go through with this thing..." Another long exhalation of breath that sounded a little incredulous. "I still can't believe you actually stumbled into it like this. I've followed it through and found nothing. I was just about to dump the whole idea...and you come up with this." And he swore softly.

Callie's thoughts were racing and leapfrogging over one another, and coherency was fast eluding her. It was an effort to concentrate long enough to complete a sentence. "Do you think—it's important?"

His hesitance was meaningful. He did not want to

build her hopes. "It's the only solid clue we have," he admitted at last. "But listen, Callie, I think you've gone about as far as you can with this thing. If Frye is involved with the Red Knights—and that's a big if—and if they know you're on to him. . . well, it could get unpleasant. Maybe you should let me see what I can find out from this end. Just keep a low profile for awhile."

"Yeah. . . sure." But Callie's eyes were narrowed on some distant object, her face taut, her brow furrowed. Her fingernails were digging into the telephone receiver.

"There's not too much more you can do anyway."

She was not aware of the lengthening silence until he prompted, "Callie?"

Callie forcefully dragged herself back to attention. "Right," she said. "Sure, you're right. There's nothing I can do."

"Okay. I'll be back with you in a couple of days. You take care of yourself, huh?"

But as Callie lowered the receiver she knew there was something she could do. And she was the only one who could do it.

Jed Frye. Sage McCormick. Code Forty-seven. "All I had to do was push a button and your whole life's story came spilling out. . ." He knew computers. He had access. He had power. He had the entire organization of Red Knights behind him. . . dissidents, traitors, criminals, and spies. Her long search was over; the end of the road was in sight. Callie had found the missing link.

Then why did she feel like crying?

Sunday was a long day. In reversal of their usual natures, Callie rose with the sun and Tandy overslept. Apparently Tandy sought escape when she was depressed; Callie sought action.

Only in this case Callie's mode of action was nothing more than a futile waste of energy. She couldn't sit still. Her pulse was racing only a step or two behind her thoughts, and the two pots of coffee she consumed before noon did nothing to calm her. She walked around the apartment, opened the blinds on a miserably dreary day, and closed them again. She turned the television on, ran through all the stations, tried to concentrate on a locally produced church service, but nothing could calm her spirit. She glanced through the Sunday paper. There was more fighting in the Middle East, bombings in Northern Ireland, guerilla warfare in Central America. . . Callie felt a cold knot forming in her chest and she quickly flipped the pages. On the local level, a seventeen-year-old boy had just been awarded a Rhodes scholarship, a missing two-year-old had been safely returned to her parents, and an outspoken conservative senator was making the university one of his stopping points on the re-election campaign trail. That article interested Callie for a time, but she could not concentrate long enough to finish it. That event was scheduled for two weeks away. Who knew what would become of her in two weeks?

She wondered what Sage was doing today.

Callie went over and over it again in her mind, analyzing it, re-examining the evidence, checking for mistakes. It had all been there from the beginning, all the hints, the clues, the bits and pieces of proof that she had needed to wind it all together. Jed Frye, renowned terrorist of the sixties, two decades later surfacing to relive the pattern of his life. Another campus, another radical group...it made perfect sense. Sage McCormick, by his own admission a radical in his youth, now a leader in his middle years. "Whoever did this," Brad had said about the computer file, "had to be pretty powerful." Just how powerful was Sage?

No wonder he had taken an interest in her. What was it he had said last night about recruitment? She had come into his class conversant in a language that automatically cast suspicion on her. Sage had taken one look at her course schedule and had seen where her interests lay, and she *had* been in every hot spot of the world for the past few years. It was not inconceivable that she could have been involved in the politics of those nations as more than just an interpreter. It was not so farfetched that he might see her as a prime candidate for persuasion to his political beliefs.

It was all there, step by step, point by point, as clear as it could be. Then why did Callie fight so hard against believing it?

She thought of the places she had been, the things she had seen. Soldiers in the streets. Curfew at six o'clock. Headlines splattered with blood. Bombs going off only yards from her window. Children dying. She had seen the results of terrorism firsthand, and she recoiled from the image. This was her country, her home, and she did not want to think things like that could happen here. Callie wanted to be safe here. She *should* be safe here. A low fury boiled within her when she thought that her way of life could be threatened by a group of radicals who thought they could change the world through violence...

But that's what her father had done. That had been the entire purpose of Jed Frye's life...blind causes, noble ideals, killing, destroying, wiping out whatever stood in his way. And she was his daughter. His blood ran through her veins. How could she sit in judgment on Sage McCormick?

Callie could not stand it any longer. She couldn't stay within the confines of this small apartment and go slowly mad. She had to get out.

The day was raw and unforgiving. The charcoal sky seemed to blend into the atmosphere, not hanging over the earth but becoming a part of it. Last night's rain lay on the dying grass and withered leaves like leftover tears, and there was not even a breeze to dry it. But far from daunting her, the ugliness of the outside world only fortified Callie. She was in sympathy with it.

Of course, there was something about the entire situation that did not ring true. Maybe it was just because Callie wanted so badly not to believe it. Maybe it had something to do with what Sage had told her last night. If his loyalty was to an anti-government faction, why hadn't he tried harder to get her to stay? Far from it, he had warned her away. There was hope in that. "I tried to walk away," he had told her, "but they wouldn't let me." He didn't want to be involved. He was not an evil person. He knew it was wrong...but still he was involved. Wasn't he?

No. Everything within her fought against believing it. There must be another explanation for Sage's behavior, another meaning to his words. Callie had overlooked something. Sage was not a criminal. He had nothing to do with terrorism or Red Knights or anything that was not strictly moral and upstanding...

And then she recalled her own words to Jerry so long ago. "If he had lived in 1776...he would have been called a patriot..."

She tilted her head back helplessly to the cruel and angry sky. None of it made sense. How could she judge?

Callie simply did not want to admit to herself that she was in love with a man who represented everything she despised.

But, of course, none of that had any bearing on the matter at hand. The point was that she had found the compass that pointed her to her father, and that compass was Sage McCormick. Callie tried to put this within the realm of logic, to wipe out her emotions, forget what she felt, and remember only what she wanted. She had spent most of her life on this soul-encompassing quest, and now the prize was hers for the grabbing. Sage McCormick could lead her to her father. All she had to do was ask.

And suppose she was wrong. Suppose, despite all evidence to the contrary, she had misjudged Sage, misinterpreted her information? If she told him who her father was, and she was wrong about Sage...what would he think of her? Wouldn't that only further confirm his suspicions about her? Callie wanted so badly for him to be innocent, but if he was, and she told him...

And if he was not. Someone had gone to a lot of trouble to protect Jed Frye, up to and including sabotaging access to a government computer. What made her think she could just walk up to Sage and ask him to point out Jed Frye for her?

And then a thought so chilling struck her that she stopped dead. Suppose he—or they—already knew? If they had any idea that Callie had come this close to finding Frye, what might they do to stop her?

She turned and started quickly back to the apartment. She couldn't go on like this. She was making herself crazy.

Tandy was up when Callie returned. She was up, but not yet dressed, and sat at the window, looking out morosely. A steaming cup of coffee was in her hand.

"Well," Callie said, nodding at the coffee cup as she shed her raincoat, "this is a switch. Aren't you the one who's always lecturing me about addiction?"

Tandy's smile was weak and mirthless as she sipped from the cup. "Might as well poison myself," she said. "Can't think of anything better to do."

Callie hung up her coat and walked slowly over to

her friend. Perhaps it was the simple softness of her nature, or perhaps it was the fact that her own problems were so overwhelming that it would be a relief to share in Tandy's petty troubles, but Callie suddenly felt like being a confidant. She settled herself into the bean-bag chair across from Tandy and said gently, "You're not still upset about your father's visit, are you?"

Tandy shrugged and took another sip of her coffee. She seemed embarrassed. "If you knew him, you'd see what there is to be upset about."

"Tandy, come on." Callie was trying hard to be sympathetic. "He can't be all that bad. I mean, he cares enough about you to come see you—"

Tandy only snorted. "Cares, nothing! He's just showing off. Any excuse to grandstand."

A puzzled frown began to form on Callie's brow, but Tandy continued bitterly, "You have no idea what the man is like. I mean, he's positively smothering. I can't remember all the times he's made me wish I'd never been born—or if I had to be, why I had to be born to him. He's made my life pure hell."

Callie tried not to let her shock at the girl's words penetrate her voice. "What on earth," she inquired softly, "could he possibly have done to make you hate him so much?"

Tandy shook her hair out of her face, her jawline rigid, her eyes hard. "Everything. Nothing." And then dropped her eyes to her cup. "Oh, hell," she muttered. "I didn't mean to make him sound like a childbeater or anything... It wasn't that. I mean, a lot of people think he's great. He sure thinks he's great.'' And she tried to laugh. The effort failed. She continued, absently drawing circles around her coffee cup, "It's just that those people don't know what it was like to live with him. I mean, all he cared about was who he was and what he represented—his family got the leftovers, if anything at all. 'Keeping up appearances,'" she mimicked in a high, sarcastic voice. Then her tone fell again. "That's all that mattered to him. What people thought. And even that wouldn't have been so bad, but he was so—so rigid. He made his own rules and we had to live by them, or else." Tandy glanced at Callie, almost shyly, then away. "As you can imagine," she said, "I've been a great disappointment to him."

Callie smiled, understanding now a little more about Tandy's eccentricities. Her friend was just rebelling against a domineering father, asserting her independence by going against the rules. Callie wondered what she would have been like if she had had a father to rebel against.

"It's just that he's so damned responsible," Tandy sighed, looking at Callie. "Do you have any idea what it's like to live in the shadow of a man who takes the whole world on his shoulders...and then expects you to help him carry it?" She shook her head and got up, crossing to the kitchen. "It's just not for me," she said, and poured her coffee into the sink. "No way."

Tandy was still far from her ebullient self, but she did seem to act a little better as she went to her room to get dressed. Callie was glad all Tandy had needed was to talk because she did not know what comfort she could have offered her. As a matter of fact the entire situation struck Callie as sadly ironic. Here was Tandy, furious because her father was coming to see her, and there was Callie, ready to put what might very well amount to her life on the line just for a chance to see her father... Tandy's father, whose only crime was that he was too responsible; Callie's father, who was the epitome of criminal irresponsibility... a trait that his daughter might very well have inherited.

Why hadn't she told Jerry about Sage McCormick? Why hadn't she told him that she could identify members of the Red Knights, that she was in a position now to infiltrate the organization and expose them all? Why hadn't she given all the information she had, all her speculation and suppositions to Jerry and let him turn it over to the authorities? That was her duty, wasn't it, as a citizen and a concerned human being? But nothing had ever stood between Callie and her mystical quest, just like nothing had ever stood in the way of Jed Frye's revolutionary ideals... not duty, not honor, not human life.

Callie went over to her desk and sat down. Slowly she took out the folded newspaper clipping that she had guarded so carefully all these years. She could remember as clear as if it were yesterday the moment her father had become a real and living entity to her.

Callie remembered her mother in the small antiseptic hospital room, at last succumbing to the life-eating organism that had eeked away her tenuous hold on life for years. They both knew she was dying. They had had plenty of time to prepare for it. But it was typical of the woman who had never paid much attention to the details of living to reveal the most important information of her daughter's life almost as an afterthought. She told Callie about the metal strong box at home—a surprising revelation in itself, for Callie had never known her mother to save anything. Then she told Callie about a man called Jed Frye with dreams and ambitions, high aspirations and limitless imagination. . . a man who wanted to change the world and set about doing it the best way he knew how. Callie had never been able to hate him. She saw only the man her mother had loved, the man who had given his genes to the woman Callie had become, but had left her without an identity. . . And she was only grateful for the discovery, partial as it might be, of that identity now.

Callie spent days after her mother's funeral gazing at the fuzzy newspaper photograph, memorizing every word in the article. She knew she should have been shocked. Instead she went to the library and researched every word that had ever been published about Jed Frye. She knew he was wrong. Everything about him was wrong. He was a criminal, a fugitive. . . but she couldn't hate him. He was her father.

She smoothed the ragged clipping on her desk absently, over and over again, like a caress. She stared

at the picture until it blurred before her eyes. So
close. . . so close.

"Oh, Daddy," she whispered, and that was when
she realized the blurriness in her eyes was tears.
They spilled down her cheeks, one drop at a time,
blotting the paper, scalding her fingers. "What am
I going to do?"

Callie went to class Monday as purely a matter of
routine; she couldn't think what else to do. She
came home afterward and spent most of the rest of
the day staring out the window, going over and over
the same circuit in her mind. She did not keep her
appointment with Sage on Tuesday. Wednesday she
did not go to class at all. It was uncharacteristic of
her to be so indecisive, so devoid of action, and
never before in her life had she been known to hide
from anything. But she was definitely hiding from
Sage. And perhaps she was hiding from the need to
make a decision.

Tandy spent a lot of time meditating and "trying
to get in touch with her true self." Brad came by,
ostensibly to inquire about Callie and to apologize
for losing her Saturday night, but he did not try
very hard to hide the fact that his real interest in the
apartment was Tandy. That was the only good
thing that had come out of this whole mess. Brad
took Tandy out for a pizza—inviting Callie to join
them, of course, and looking grateful when she refused—and Tandy returned much cheered. Callie
was glad.

About the party Brad said, "I'm sorry for taking
you to a place like that—I didn't realize it was going

to be so wild. I guess you cut out before it got too heavy, huh?''

Callie did not want to talk about it. She did not even want to remember it. She nodded.

''Well, I did, too. I looked for you, but I couldn't find you. I didn't know anybody there anyway,'' he added. ''The guy who invited me didn't even show. Weird bunch of folks,'' he reflected, and Callie was only relieved that whoever had invited Brad had apparently failed in his mission, too.

Callie spent a lot of time at her desk, touching the newspaper article, staring at the man in the photograph as though sheer will power could make him come to life. She could not go backwards and was afraid to go forward. And she could not go to the one man who could tell her what to do.

The evidence was certainly stacked high against Sage, but perhaps it was her innate tendency to defend the underdog that made the overwhelming evidence all the more reason for believing in his innocence. Okay, so he happened to be in possession of an incendiary rag sheet. Anyone could have gotten hold of one of those. And maybe his political philosophies were a little offbeat...was that any reason to condemn a man as a traitor? People were entitled to their opinions, anything less would be fascism. And he happened to keep company with suspicious types...so did she, for that matter. She had been at that party, too. Sage had as much reason to suspect Callie as she did him...as he had made abundantly clear the last time they met.

As for the computer... She couldn't explain

that. But how could she be expected to? She knew
nothing about computers and there could be a
dozen technical and very plausible reasons for the
deletion of Sage's file that she had no way of knowing. Brad could have made a mistake running the
program. It could be a flaw in the system. It could
be something very simple and perfectly explainable,
and all of this worry could be for nothing.

Going by strict logic, things did not look good for
Sage. But the feel was not right. Something about it
was a little off-key...

And Callie had to justify to herself what the big
deal about the Red Knights was anyway. She had no
concrete proof that anyone she had met at that party was a member of the organization, or that it did
in fact actually exist. She was going entirely on cir-
cumstantial evidence. But even if the group did exist
here on campus and even if Sage was associated
with them...what had they done to be condemned
for? Callie had never even heard of them before
talking to Jerry. If they had engaged in any overtly
criminal activities, surely Jerry would have told her.
No bombings, no murders, no kidnappings...
They were just an organization of people who held
alternative political viewpoints, and who was Callie
to judge them? Who was she to judge anyone on
morality or politics?

Although starting to feel a little better, she still
did not know what she was going to do. But the situation was looking somewhat brighter. It was only
the cynicism of a long life of searching and not finding that made Callie suspect the worst of every-

thing, but perhaps the fact that she had not been able to talk herself into believing the worst of Sage was a sign of hope.

Or maybe it was a sign of foolishness.

And then on Thursday afternoon Callie responded to an imperious knock on the front door and stood face to face with Sage McCormick. And she knew that the chance for making her own decision had just been taken out of her hands.

Chapter Ten

Callie looked at him, lean and capable in jeans and a hooded sweatshirt, the curly hair, the definitive face, the crystal eyes, and she felt as though she were coming home. Everything about him reached out to her; everything within her responded to him. She could not remember doubting him; she could not relate to the fears that had haunted her the past four days. Although she tried to guard against it, something within her beat back reason and let emotion emerge. All Callie cared about was that he was here; all she felt was that he could make everything right. And all she wanted to do was to step into his arms.

But she said instead, trying very hard to keep the happiness and the relief out of her voice, "What—what are you doing here?"

"I have brought," he announced, and swept past her into the room, "the mountain to Mohammed. Where shall we set up?"

Sage glanced around the room; then, without waiting for her answer, he proceeded to her desk. Callie followed him a little uncertainly.

"I get paid whether you learn anything or not," Sage informed her, unpacking his briefcase. "Now I can't control what you learn, but I can do my best to see that you get your money's worth. You've missed two lessons and a class, but you still have a chance to catch up. Unless. . ." And now he looked at her pointedly. "You aren't really interested in getting a degree at all?"

It was a challenge, an invitation to confession, but it came too quickly and too unexpectedly for Callie to respond. She stammered, "Of—of course, I am. It's just that. . ."

But Sage was not interested in her explanations; he knew them already. He interrupted brusquely, "Let's get to work then. We have a lot of time to make up." He opened his textbook and sat behind her desk.

Callie was in a daze. She could not believe that he actually expected her to sit and concentrate on Russian verbs, but as a matter of fact, he gave her no choice. The questions and assignments he fired at her demanded her full attention, allowing no time for wondering or reluctance, firmly and pointedly establishing her role as student and his as teacher. Did he know the mental and emotional turmoil she had been going through the past few days? Hadn't he guessed the reasons she had avoided his classes? Was this his way of telling her he had washed his hands of her and her personal concerns? And if so, why? Or. . . could it be that his intense drilling and demand for her concentration was intentionally directed to take her mind off weightier concerns, to give her a chance to step back and put things in perspective before she drove herself crazy?

Whatever his motivation, it worked. For an hour or longer he kept her encapsulated in a world where nothing intruded but the sound of his voice and the orders he gave her. And for the first time in days, Callie felt reason, normalcy, and order begin to return to her world. Sage was here, and everything was just as it had always been. No problem was quite so insurmountable after all. Nothing had changed. Sage was the same as he had always been, and no choices confronted Callie that had not been there all along. She wasn't so afraid any longer. She could deal with it now.

A long time of silence had passed while Callie was rewriting a paragraph Sage had dictated to her and corrected, and when she looked up to hand it to him, she was surprised to find him smiling gently at her. "What do you say," he invited, taking the paper without glancing at it, "we go get some dinner?"

Callie did not hesitate, not even for a second. Later she could analyze her reasons for acceptance as being strictly logical: she needed to know what Sage's real purpose in coming here had been. She could not refuse an opportunity to feel him out for more information about the Red Knights because there was always a chance that he might talk more about himself and the people he was involved with, and he was the only link she had to her father. But right then the only thing Callie was thinking about was that she wanted to be with him. And she could not help returning his smile. "I'll get my coat," she said.

Callie went into the bedroom to brush her hair and exchange her house slippers for more weather-worthy shoes, but she did not bother changing out of her jeans and sweater. She was almost afraid that if she lingered too long, he might disappear. She came back into the living room pulling on her down-filled parka just as Sage was packing up his briefcase, and for a moment—just the briefest part of a second—she hesitated. His face was drawn into a concentrated scowl; his attention appeared to be fixed upon something on her desk. But as soon as he heard her come in, that troubled look vanished as though it had never been. Sage glanced up at her and snapped his briefcase closed. "Ready?" he inquired, and there was nothing at all in his tone or expression to account for that brief twist of alarm Callie had felt when she first entered the room.

The last time they had been together it had been dark and wet and ugly. Today the light was dying from a sky that was as brilliant as Sage's eyes. Gold lingered on the tips of leaves and formed auras around cars and buildings. The day was cold, but not threatening. And inside the sun-heated Volvo, it was warm.

And then, settling into the seat beside Sage, Callie had her first clear and coherent thought since he had walked in her door. *Do you realize what you're doing? You've just gotten into the car with a man who could be a wanted criminal...* But the thought had no power over her. It didn't frighten her, it didn't make her suspicious, it didn't put her on guard. It simply didn't matter. And she felt a burden lift from her with that realization that was long overdue. It simply didn't matter.

And she wasn't even surprised when, as he pulled the car out into the street, Sage said, "I didn't really come over today out of a burning concern over your Russian grades."

Callie looked at him calmly. "Why did you come?"

His attention was fixed on maneuvering the car into the stream of traffic and he did not look at her. "I thought," he said simply, "that you might need to talk."

That was her opening. Would he tell her, if she asked, about Jed Frye and the Red Knights? Would he tell her about computer Code Forty-seven and what exactly it was that he had done on the border of Czechoslovakia that he was so ashamed of? Callie sensed very strongly that he would...if she asked. So she did not ask.

That was when Callie knew why her instincts to trust Sage were so strong. He had never kept secrets from her. Sometimes he was cryptic, sometimes reluctant; but when the need arose, he was open with her at whatever cost to himself. It was Callie who had refused to be completely honest with him. She wanted that to be different now; she wanted for once to open up and share completely with him and put all this suspicion and mistrust behind them— but she didn't know how to begin. She didn't want to use Sage for her own purposes, not now, not when she was just discovering how important he was to her. . .

She turned her eyes away from his profile to study her hands. And she answered very softly, "Not now. Maybe. . . later."

He simply looked at her, a brief glance that acknowledged and consented to her request. The silence said more than words could. Sage understood.

And Callie was grateful.

They did not talk as Sage drove slowly through winding residential streets flanked with double-parked cars, but it was an easy silence, not strained. Callie absorbed the brilliance of a fiery sunset and the reflection of autumn foliage and the still, lazy afternoon, and she did not realize until Sage had turned the car into a driveway that they were not heading toward the highway and its established eating facilities but had stopped in a residential neighborhood only a couple of blocks from the campus.

Callie glanced at him, and he grinned, a sudden and beautifully disarming gesture that all but took her breath away. "Two days before payday," he answered the unspoken question, "where else can I afford to take you?"

Sage got out of the car and Callie hesitated for only another moment before opening her door and stepping out. The house before her was one of the most adorable stone cottages she had ever seen. It might once have been a gate house on a large estate, or it might have been modeled after one, but it re-

minded Callie of the house Hansel and Gretel had
found in the woods. It was, like all other houses on
the street, set back on the lot and surrounded by live
oaks and elms. In the front yard, straight across the
driveway from where Sage had parked, there was a
swing that soon would have to be taken in and protected from the elements. Flower beds, now filled
with pinestraw and rotting leaves, formed ovals on
either side of the front stoop, and several brave yellow chrysanthemums survived in a raised stone bed
surrounding one sturdy oak tree in the center of the
lawn. The lawn itself was badly in need of raking,
but Callie liked the sound and the smell of crunching leaves under her feet, and the carpet of color
only added to the charm of the little house.

Sage led her up the three stone steps and un-
locked a cathedral-style door, gesturing her inside.
Callie caught her breath as she stepped across the
threshold and Sage touched a switch that illuminated an amber-globed lamp by the doorway. It was
lovely. Callie did not know what she had expected
from Sage, but somehow this she had never imagined.

The floors were gleaming hardwood with colorful
red and orange and blue scatter rugs gaily drawing
together the warmth of the room. The motif was
Early American, with generous use of calico and
denim in the furnishings. There was a hunting scene
over the fireplace and wood stacked on the hearth.
The sofa and chairs drawn up before it looked comfortable and well-used, and a worn red-and-blue
afghan folded on a footstool invited Callie to cud-

dle up before the fireplace and relax. Magazines were stuffed to capacity in a brass rack by one of the chairs, and a tall bookcase held everything from adventure paperbacks to high-school trophies, all in a delightfully intriguing clutter. A spiral staircase ascended from one corner, and upstairs was a sleeping loft guarded by a balcony rail that overlooked half of the room. It was the most delightful house Callie had ever been in, warm and charming and filled with personality. Everything about it said that the person who lived here cared, and Callie loved it.

But the best part was not the warm, country-cozy decor, the haphazard mismatching of furniture, the bright colors, or even the quaintly uneven stone foyer or the wonderful sleeping loft. The best part was the scent that wrapped around her the moment she stepped inside, the scent of something delicious and bubbly and mouth-watering cooking in the kitchen.

Callie breathed deeply, letting the aroma mingle with the atmosphere of the place and carry her away to fantasies of gluttony and indulgent comfort. "Ummm," she murmured, "What is that?"

"I've had a pot roast simmering all day," Sage informed her, hanging his briefcase on a hook by the door. "Another very excellent reason for not taking you to a noisy, crowded, high-priced restaurant tonight."

Callie's eyes widened. "You cook?"

He looked amused as he slipped her coat off her shoulders. "Some people do that, you know."

"But—I mean..." She followed him as he

passed through another small room to the kitchen, switching on lights as he went. "A whole roast for just yourself? Why bother?"

He shrugged as he touched the final light and a small, spotless, red-and-white checked kitchen sprang into view. "Because I like to."

Callie wandered around while he checked the roast, smiling to herself, running her hand lightly along the bright red counter tops, touching quilted toaster and blender covers, absorbing it all, loving it all. The cabinets had mullioned glass doors and the shelves were lined with red checked paper that matched the curtains over the window and café-style door. She noticed that a lot of his glasses sported cartoon characters. On the refrigerator door was a magnetized apple from which was suspended the note, "Buy Milk." The scribble pad by the telephone was filled with phone numbers, half-finished grocery lists, and aimless doodles. Every corner of this room, just like the room she had left, was filled with him. It was a home, and it warmed Callie to her very toes.

"Perfect timing," Sage pronounced, and slid the roasting pan out of the oven. Heat seeped from the open door and gently fanned the small room. "I hope you're hungry."

"I am now." Callie was glowing with contentment. She had never felt so warm or comfortable in any place before. What had he done to make her feel so? Perhaps nothing, she decided finally. Perhaps all he had to do was walk into a room, any room, to make her feel as though she had found a home.

Callie volunteered to set the dining room table while Sage transferred the succulent roast and steaming vegetables to a serving platter, and she was delighted to notice that none of his plates matched. He refused, however, to let her pour the burgundy he had just opened into jelly glasses, and after much searching, he finally found two goblets.

Sage lit a fat blue candle that gave off a jasmine scent and placed it on the polished oak table beneath a wagon-wheel chandelier. And Callie discovered that he could, indeed, cook, as they sat down to eat.

"Marvelous," she murmured in wide-eyed appreciation with the first bite. "Where did you learn to cook?"

Sage tried to disguise his pleasure in her compliment with a negligent shrug. "My mom. She owned a little homestyle restaurant in the town where I grew up—still does, as a matter of fact. All of us kids learned to cook as soon as we could reach the stove on a stepladder."

"All of you?" Suddenly Callie was filled with curiosity about him, and it was more than just an idle interest—it was a need to know and share in his life, to become a part of all that had gone on before with him. "How many?"

"Three brothers and a sister," he answered, and it was the most natural thing in the world that he should go on to tell her about his childhood in a town of ten thousand, about his father's auto body repair shop, his youngest brother's adventures on the rodeo circuit, and his sister's husband and fami-

ly. . . filling her hungry soul with the anecdotes and
escapades of a normal, everyday family, the kind
she had never had.

Two days ago she would not have believed she
would be sitting at Sage's table over a home-cooked
meal, basking in the glow of his cozy home, and relaxing in the pleasure of his company. Even now
Callie could not understand how she had gotten to
this point. The suspicions she had had, the fears
that had gnawed at her, seemed so far away now. . .
and so inappropriate to this time, to this place.
With Sage she could forget who she was and what
she wanted. When she was with Sage all Callie
wanted was within the embrace of her arms, and
nothing else seemed important.

As though they had been doing it all their lives,
they cleared the table together and stacked the
dishes in the dishwasher. Sage poured the last of the
wine into their glasses and held her hand as they
walked back into the living room. Callie sank down
into the foamy cushions of the sofa as Sage lit a
fire.

"Your house," she said softly, looking around
her, "is wonderful. It's exactly the type of place I
would want."

A flame caught and kindled, lapping a blue-and-
red glow around the freshly stacked logs, and Sage
got up and came over to her, smiling. "It's exactly
the kind of place I've always wanted," he admitted,
sitting beside her. "When I came to the university
and decided to settle down, the first thing I did was
buy this house. I've spent five years giving it that

lived-in look," he added wryly, lifting himself a little to toss aside the magazine upon which he had been sitting.

Callie laughed softly and sipped her wine. Her eyes still glowed with taking it all in—the reflection of the fire dancing off the gleaming wood floors, the warm pine-paneled walls, the cluttered bookshelves, and chintz throw cushions. "I mean it, Sage; it's just perfect." And she added as she glanced at him, "I never would have thought you were the domestic type."

"Oh?" He rested his arm along the back of the sofa, and his fingers began to play with her hair. "What type did you think I was?"

"Oh..." Callie lowered her eyes to her glass, watching her reflection there for a moment before casting a teasing glance his way. "The swashbuckling type," she decided.

His eyes caught the play of the flames and blended it into a subtle, fascinating, multicolored dance of sparks and shadows as he laughed. "I've been that, too," he admitted. "But all that swinging around on chandeliers was hard on my back."

When she laughed, Sage's eyes lightened and widened with pleasure and then slowly began to soften. His expression at that moment was as tender as the caress of his fingers on the back of her neck, and the laughter died on Callie's lips, to be subtly replaced by a sense of growing wonder and anticipation. "You look happy, Callie," he said. "It seems like I've waited forever to see you really happy."

"I am," she answered him softly. Happier, perhaps, than she had ever been in her life, and for no
good reason. No reason at all...

His hand cupped gently around her neck, warm
strong fingers guiding her to him; he leaned down
and kissed her. It was gentle, intimate, loving, and
reassuring, a brief touching and tasting, a reminder
of things more perfect. "It's good to have you here,
Callie," he whispered, and his eyes were shaded
lamps that illuminated everything, revealed nothing.

Sage removed her glass from her hand, and their
lips met again. Again the sweet weakness, again the
building yearning, again she felt herself begin to
flow into him, and it was right. Just perfectly right.
She tasted his tongue and the richness of wine. She
felt the heat that molded her into him. And she did
not fight it. Tonight, just tonight, she wanted to
believe that this could be real and that here with this
man she had at last found her home.

Callie could feel the tension in his muscles and
the throbbing of his pulse beneath her fingers that
caressed his neck. She could feel the mounting heat
in his face and through the fabric of his sweatshirt.
His fingers drifted down her back and tightened
there as though restraining restlessness, and then
suddenly he pulled away. "Callie." His voice was
husky and his face rough against her cheek. "We
need to talk."

No. Not tonight. Tonight let her have just this
one perfect moment... Her hand was trembling as
she touched his cheek, exploring the warmth and

the dampness there. And she said simply, "No," and guided his mouth back to hers.

It was all Callie had ever dreamed of and all she had ever wanted, making love with this man. It was slow and beautiful and dreamily sensuous. It was the touch of sensitive fingers and a dewy rain of delicate kisses; then it was a flame of passion that blotted out reason, and it was the gentle lowering of that inferno to a basking glow. It was the discovery of the artwork of his body, smooth skin and taut muscles, feathery lashes and silken curls. It was being carried up a winding staircase while the world faded out dizzily below; it was the feel of cool linen against her heated skin while he slowly undressed her. It was sensation and imagination, shadow and light. The flickering of a candle at the bedside. The glow of wooden beams overhead. The clean, lean lines of Sage's chest and abdomen as he slowly pulled the sweatshirt over his head. The dark intensity of his eyes as his face drew close to hers. Her face cupped in his hands, her world swallowed up in the endless depths of those eyes as their bodies joined. Pain and passion, reaching and touching, wanting and grasping, desperation and despair...they knew it all, they shared it all. All barriers between them dissolved. Truths and half-truths, secrets and evasions, who was wrong and who was right, none of it mattered as they opened all for one another and became one. Together they sought, together they found, and together they reached the end of that long and empty journey. It felt like coming home.

Callie lay tangled in Sage's arms, her mind empty and her heart full. The only sound was his quiet breathing, the only motion that of his fingers as he drew the strands of her hair over his shoulder in a soothing, repetitive motion. It had happened suddenly, but it seemed as though she had been waiting for this the whole of her life. Whatever the future held, she would not regret this moment. It was all she was meant for and all she had come to be, and nothing stirred within her but contentment.

After a long time the movement of Sage's fingers stopped. He simply held her and she held him and she wanted nothing else. No words, no comfort, no questions, no reassurances. The sweet mindlessness of perfection was engulfing her, and all she wanted was to stay like this forever.

Then Sage said quietly, ''Tell me about Jed Frye, Callie.''

Chapter Eleven

The candle sparked and flared, shadows danced crazily on the walls, and dripping wax hissed. For a moment Callie did not move. And then, very slowly, as though she were moving under water, she sat up, dragging the sheet with her for shelter while she looked dully around the room for her clothes.

And Sage said nothing behind her. She could hear him breathing; she could feel him waiting, as steady and alert as a jungle animal who can wait all day for an unwary prey to fall into his trap. Callie saw her clothes lying on the floor at the foot of the bed beneath the tumble of a down comforter. But she could not make herself move to retrieve them. She could not imagine herself possessing the energy, the purpose, the strength it would take to get dressed and walk out the door. The pain had not started yet. All she felt was numb.

And all she could say was, flatly, "How did you know about him?"

It was a redundant question for she knew the answer already. Yet there was no surprise when he answered simply, "The article on your desk. It's old; you've obviously kept it with you a long time. Why?"

Callie wanted to believe him. She wanted very badly to believe that the first time he had ever heard of Jed Frye was this afternoon when he read a clipping she had carelessly left lying about. And maybe that was why she answered, reaching slowly for her sweater at the foot of the bed, "He's my father."

It was that simple. In all these years she had told only one other person, and only then because it was the only way she could get him to help. She did not expect Sage to help now. She did not expect anything. It was just, strangely, a relief to tell him, to have it out in the open. All her secrets were his now, and it was good to stop hiding.

Sage was silent for a very long time. He was shocked, of course, Callie reflected dimly as she pulled on her sweater. This was not what he had expected at all. . .

And then he said softly, "Well, that explains a lot."

She had to turn and look at him. He had not moved. He still lay there, one arm crooked behind his head, the other stretched over her pillow where she had left it. And his expression in the shadowy golden light was gentle, sensitive, thoughtful. Not condemning. Not suspicious. Not even excited.

Callie's voice was a little hoarse. "Like what?"

"You." He was watching her in the flickering candlelight, his expression soft, his words easy and understanding. "South America, Mexico, the Caribbean. . .all the places a fugitive might hide. It's been a long road for you, hasn't it, Callie?''

Then the pain started. Callie tilted her head back, elongating aching throat muscles that threatened to choke off her very breath, willing back the scalding tears. Why did it surprise her to hear it put into words like that? Hadn't she known all along that those exotic locations, important sounding titles, a high-paying job—that all of it was designed purely to put her in places her father might have been, to let her breathe the air he might have breathed, and to touch the things he might have touched, and perhaps, by some chance, to find a sign of him. . . something that would lead her to him. It was no surprise.

Sage lightly touched her arm. Callie could not move. She held herself rigid with the pain, afraid to let go, afraid of what would begin if she gave into it. Tears were flooding her chest and throbbing in her head, but she would not let them reign. Yes, it had been a long road, and it had lead her here. . . Then why did it feel like the end of hope?

Sage's fingers lightly stroked her arm, offering comfort, not condemnation. If ever there was a time for her to be frightened, this was it. Sage held the power over her now. He knew who she was and what she sought. He could either help her or destroy her. But Callie was not frightened. She was only hurting. And she was not prepared for what he said next.

''Why,'' he asked simply, ''didn't you tell me before?''

Callie bowed her head. She couldn't fight it any more. The tears spilled over and her voice was thick and trembling with the power of them. "B—because," she half whispered, "I was a—afraid..." Afraid of what he would think of her before she knew who he was, afraid of what he would do afterwards...afraid of trusting the fragility of a dream to hands other than her own.

There was a poignancy in the silence, a stillness and an expectancy. Sage's next words seemed almost to come without breath. "And now?" he prompted softly.

"Now..." The words flowed from her as uncontrollably as the tears. "Now—it's too late. I—love you..."

Slowly, gently, he gathered her into his arms. His breath fluttered over her shoulder and her tears wet his chest. "And that," he whispered gently, smoothing back her hair, "is the key to the whole thing, isn't it? Loving each other, trusting each other... It takes away our common sense and makes us do things we'll probably regret..." Then she felt his lips on her face, his arms tightening around her with sudden ferocity. "Don't regret this, Callie," he said huskily. "Don't make me regret it..."

But the plea, too, came too late. If regret it she must, then regret it she would, but for tonight she would hold on tight to the only thing that had ever been worth having, for tonight she would let him take her pain and soothe her fears, and she would let herself feel safe in his arms. Tomorrow would be soon enough to face the consequences.

And tomorrow did come, slowly and in reluctant stages. Morning light filtered through steamy windows, first gray, then yellow, then finally in shafts of unrelenting white. Callie watched it arrive without dread, snuggled in the warmth of a fluffy patchwork comforter, huddled against the heat of Sage's nakedness. His hand was resting on her thigh, his breathing soft and even on the pillow next to hers. His limbs were strong and perfect next to hers, and she wanted to touch them, ankles, calves, lean thighs and hard buttocks, the spareness of his waist, and the light furring of hair across his chest... She wanted his arms to tighten around her and smother her in his embrace. She wanted to imprint every part of him on her and remember it forever.

Last night they had made love again, and the bonding had sealed something between them that defied the powers of Callie's mind that threatened to tear them apart. Last night there had been wine and candlelight and need, all of which were very good explanations for the irrational series of events that had led her to his bed, led her to a confession with no recriminations and no regrets. But last night there had been something else, and it was something that would not crumple under the weight of justification nor fade before the harsh light of morning. Callie loved Sage, and love did not need answers to make it right.

Last night Callie had realized that all her decisions had been made for her. And was it so shocking? Sage McCormick, radical, terrorist, traitor to all she loved and prized... a carbon copy of her father. And it was Callie's destiny to be by his side, hating herself and loving him, wherever there were bombs to be thrown and governments to be deposed, where children cried in the streets and liberation was the sound of breaking glass...to be with him wherever he asked her to go. It was in her blood to love this man. She had never had any choice.

Callie felt, rather than saw, Sage's gaze upon her. She turned her head to meet eyes that were thoughtful and aware, dark with the clarity of her secrets...eyes that studied her and examined her but made no judgments. Today they would have to talk, they both knew that; but they both also felt the need to postpone it as long as possible.

Sage smiled, slowly, and it seemed to Callie an almost painful gesture. His lips brushed her cheek and his hand moved along her thigh, brushing her bare hip, seeking beneath the sweater she had never removed to tickle her spine. She wanted to make love to him, and she knew he wanted it too. But his fingers tightened for just a brief embrace upon the small of her back. He kissed her again, lightly, and sat up. "I'll put some coffee on," he said.

Callie watched him as he got out of bed and reached for the jeans he had discarded last night. She could see his flesh prickle as it met the cool air of the room, and she followed with her eyes the beautiful symmetry of his back, the tapering of his waist, the firm rise of his buttocks as he pulled the jeans upward. Sage reached for his sweatshirt and pulled it over his head; then he returned to her, sitting beside her and touching her face lightly with his hand. His expression had become very tender. "Are you all right this morning, Callie?" he inquired soberly.

Callie nodded. "Yes," she answered. And it was true. "I really am."

Her fingers linked with his for a moment; then he smiled and brought their joined hands to his lips. "That sweater looks like it has about done its duty," he pointed out, an amused glance flickering over the crushed and rumpled angora. "There's a sweatshirt in that top drawer over there, and if you want to take a shower, there are towels in the closet in the bathroom. Anything in particular you'd like for breakfast?"

"Anything but yogurt!" she replied and was surprised at how easy it was to laugh. The easy response in his eyes caught at her heart and made it soar.

He kissed her fingers once more and released them. "One yogurt-free breakfast coming up. Come down when you're ready."

The aromas of coffee and bacon drifted up to Callie as she stepped out of the shower, filling her with contentment and anticipation. It was Friday morning and neither of them had classes today; it was the beginning of their long romantic weekend... Somehow, sometime during this weekend questions would have to be asked, answers given, decisions faced. Callie knew that. But it didn't worry her any longer. Because in this place, in the shelter and protection of the man she loved, surely nothing bad could happen.

The furnace had been turned up, and Callie was not cold as she crossed back to the bedroom wrapped in a fluffy bathsheet. She heard Sage call upstairs, "Coffee's ready!" and she shouted back happily, "In a minute!"

Callie slid open the top drawer of his bureau, lifting stacks of neatly folded sweaters and T-shirts for the sweatshirt he had offered. And then she stopped, staring, a cold numbness starting in the tips of her fingers and penetrating all the way down to her toes. For there, nestled between a cable-knit sweater and a screen-printed T-shirt, was a gun.

And without warning, everything suddenly became very clear to Callie. The dazed euphoria of the night faded away; the innocence of the simple truth dissolved into something harsh and ugly. She did not know why, but something about the sight of that weapon brought everything into sharp and unyielding focus, and the sensation was like finding a snake nestled within a bouquet of roses.

She stared at it for a long time. This was not a small handgun, the kind the businessmen Callie used to work for carried for protection, the kind that could disable at close range with a small slug and good aim. This one was heavy, long-barreled, iron-black, undecorated. It was the kind of gun that could blow a man's head off at fifty yards. It was the kind people used for serious killing.

Whom did she think she was fooling? So the Red Knights were not a threat, they did not plot violence, they were simply a group of kids with unusual politics... *Whom did she think she was fooling?*

The candlelight night and the golden morning swirled and dissolved around her like a leftover dream, leaving something cold and hard in the pit of her stomach, something that spread through her body until she felt as though she were composed of the same unbendable iron that had fashioned the weapon before her. She felt ill, but she also felt strong. It was time to face the truth.

She came downstairs dressed in her jeans and her own sweater; Sage turned as she entered the kitchen. And the smile died on his lips as he looked at her.

Callie walked over to the bar and sat down on one of the two vinyl-covered stools. Sage turned silently and began to pour coffee. His expression was very blank as he brought her coffee cup to her. He merely watched her and waited.

Callie warmed her icy hands on the cup, but nothing could warm her inside. There was pain... oh, there was pain. *Talk to me, Sage,* she pleaded silently. *Lie to me; I'll believe anything. Tell me the truth if there's no other choice, but don't let these secrets keep us apart any longer*... She met Sage's gaze without flinching, and she said, "Jed Frye is on this campus, isn't he?"

Sage dropped his eyes to his coffee cup, and that was her answer. Something within Callie rolled and twisted, but she kept her voice steady. "And you know who he is," she stated flatly.

Sage looked at her. He did not have to lie. The truth was in his eyes.

Her voice was tight, her fingers cramped on the cup. "Will you tell me who he is?"

Sage tasted his coffee, then turned to the counter to add more milk. Still not a flicker of expression crossed his face as he looked back at her. "What would you do if you found him, Callie?" he asked simply. His tone was almost disinterested. "Turn him in? Put him on the run again? Or..." Still nothing in his face or his voice. "Maybe you have a more concrete use for his—shall we say—talents?"

Callie didn't answer. She couldn't. All this time she had thought all she wanted from her father was simply to meet him, to touch him, to know he was real, but Sage was demanding that she face the fact that it was more complicated than that. Could she really walk up to the man and say, "Hello, I'm your daughter," and expect it to end there? What would she do? Could she join with Frye just as she had been willing, only hours ago, to join with Sage? Could she turn her own father in? No more than she could turn in the man who stood before her, putting his secrets between her and a choice she could not make...

And then suddenly Sage's face tightened. He put down his coffee cup in an abrupt movement that spilled half of it on the countertop. "I think I'd better take you home, Callie," he said quietly, "before you say something I don't want to hear."

They did not speak during the short drive back to Callie's apartment. The morning was obscenely bright and colorful, a riot of cheer and welcome, but to Callie it looked like something preparing to die. Sage stopped the car before her building and turned to look at her. Everything in Callie's heart was drawn toward the darkness in his eyes, the lines on his face, and she forcefully pushed her depressing thoughts to the back of her mind. He said quietly, looking at her, "It's funny. I guess all my life I knew there would come a time when I would have to make this decision... But I never thought it would be like this." Then, very lightly, he touched her cheek. His fingers were cold. "I guess what it boils down to is..." And the smile that twisted at his lips was bitter as he quoted softly, " 'I could not love you half so much, dear, loved I not honor more.' "

For a moment their eyes clung, and it was a moment in which promises could have been made, secrets opened, destinies changed. But then Sage turned away, and Callie was glad.

She did not know much about honor, but she did know about love. And it was love that gave her the strength to open that door and walk away from him without looking back.

Chapter Twelve

A week had passed in such a drudgery of normal routine that Callie felt she was walking in a surrealistic nightmare. She went to class, she went to the library, she came home. She saw Sage but he did not look at her. He was the one who had canceled out her last two private lessons through an impersonal note delivered to Callie by his secretary. Tandy and Brad were out together almost every night. Life went on, but Callie was suspended somewhere in the middle of it all, caught in an emotional void.

She didn't answer the phone. Jerry called and left a message for her with Tandy, but she ignored it. The search, as far as Callie was concerned, was over. She had not found what she expected, nor perhaps even what she wanted, but she had found her answer. And the answer was that she simply did not want to know. The victory was not worth the fight.

Callie did not know whether she could continue to stay at this university, seeing Sage every day, knowing that her father was somewhere only steps away, and knowing that the two of them were stirring up an inferno that could at any moment explode into a life-consuming flame... That was something she avoided thinking about. She knew that she could not stay here, pretending to ignore the man that she loved, facing her conscience day after day, and knowing that each moment she lingered she was in danger of being drawn into a web of violence and destruction from which there was no escape... knowing that if ever once Sage held out his hand to her she would place hers within it and there would be no turning back.

But now her life was a void, a cup without a bottom, meaningless and purposeless. She went through the motions mechanically, but she was not living.

Early on Friday afternoon Callie answered the insistent rapping at the door, annoyed with Tandy for being late again. Tandy and Brad were going to hear Senator Stevens's speech, and Callie knew that Brad had told her he would pick her up at two. It was now five after, and Tandy was still in her bedroom.

"I'll get her, Brad," Callie said, motioning him inside.

"Aren't you going?" Brad questioned. "Man, you should see the crowd. Good thing it didn't rain—they never could have gotten all those people in the auditorium."

Callie smiled weakly and shook her head, starting for Tandy's bedroom. "I'm not in much of a mood for crowds," she told him.

Tandy was lying on the bed, staring up at the ceiling, and she answered dully before Callie could even question, "I'm not going. You go with Brad, will you? Tell him I'm sorry."

"But why not?" Callie came over to her. "Are you sick? What's wrong?"

Tandy sat up, turning away from her. "I'm just not going, okay? Just leave me alone."

Once again it was her roommate's childishness that nudged Callie out of her own apathy. Sometimes the little annoyances were the most powerful of all. "I am not going out there," she said firmly, her eyes narrowing, "and tell Brad you've stood him up without a good reason. So you'd better have one."

And suddenly Tandy turned on her, her face streaked with pain and her eyes dark with raw emotion. "He's my father!" she cried. "Jonathan Stevens is my father and I can't—I *will not*—"

And that was when something within Callie snapped. She simply couldn't accept it, this child's rejection of her father simply because he was a public figure who had devoted more of his life to his country than to his daughter . . . She could not accept the rejection for any reason. It was cruel, it was unfair, that this spoiled girl should turn her back on the man who had fathered her when Callie had given the best of her life for a man who never knew she existed . . .

Callie grabbed Tandy's arm and jerked her to her feet. The fury and the determination on Callie's face wiped all traces of self-pity from Tandy's and left it only stunned. "You're going," Callie said lowly, and Tandy was too nonplussed to object.

Callie might have felt some shame or regret for her uncharacteristic behavior as she walked with Brad and Tandy across the crowded campus; she would not remember. Brad chattered cheerfully and Tandy was sullen; the sky was studded with translucent white clouds and the leaves were crimson and yellow. There was noise and activity as they approached the west campus and edged their way toward the grandstand. Callie might have tried to make conversation in a roundabout way of apology to Tandy, but she didn't remember it. The only thing she did remember clearly was seeing Sage McCormick standing on the outskirts of the crowd on the opposite side of the speaker's stand from Callie. Perhaps fifty bodies separated them, but when their eyes met, the distance closed and Callie could feel his lips, his breath, the strength of his arms... And then he turned away.

Then there was a moment when everything was very clear to Callie, yet strangely disjointed. The blurred words of introduction that blared over the microphone washed over her, but the applause was deafeningly clear. She felt Tandy stiffen beside her, and she saw the distinguished white-haired gentleman rise and approach the lectern. Callie remembered thinking how genial he looked, and she heard the words, "Good afternoon ladies and gentlemen..."

And that was when everything went into slow-motion and blended together, until afterwards Callie would never be sure what she had actually seen and what had been brought to her by way of film clips. She felt, rather than heard, a murmur of horror and surprise that spread backwards to her through the crowd like a slow-moving ripple in a pond. She saw the dark-haired young man with a droopy mustache and curly hairdo rise up out of the crowd and steady a pistol with both hands, aimed toward the grandstand.

The explosion went on and on, not a single sound but a multitude of sounds that rang and echoed down the corridors of time and would live forever in the minds of those who witnessed it. It was Dallas, it was Rome, it was the streets of New York, it was Cairo and Mobile and every place in between, every man who had ever fallen beneath the senseless destiny of one bullet that could change the world. It was a fine mist of red and a lone figure crumpling to the ground, it was a roar of horror and a rush of movement and a high, piercing plea in Callie's ear that screamed over and over again, "Daddy! Daddy!"

The gun flew and turned in the air in one final brilliant display of slow-motion cinematography before everything rushed into a composite of action and noise and color: Blue uniforms tackling the man before he could run, the platform covered with men in three-piece suits and drawn pistols, pushing and shoving, people falling and running, and that scream over and over again, blotting out Callie's brain. She saw Brad's white face and Tandy's wild eyes, and she felt the rake of nails as she struggled to hold the girl back; she was aware of Brad's taking them both in his arms and pulling them away, but the screaming wouldn't stop, the screaming just wouldn't stop...

But through it all, the horror and the confusion, the movement and the noise, the terror and the pain, only one memory remained inexorably clear for Callie. That was when she saw Sage McCormick, hands in pockets, face hard and eyes cold, turn very deliberately and walk away.

It was the evening of the second day, cold and misty. Callie had spent almost the entire forty-eight hours in the hospital waiting room, existing on coffee and doughnuts and a few hours sleep snatched on hard chairs and lumpy sofas. She had not felt right about leaving Tandy before now. Senator Stevens was in satisfactory condition, recuperating from the bullet that had nicked his lung, and Tandy was with him. Brad had been a faithful visitor at the hospital, although visibly shaken both by the events and by the revelation that the Senator was Tandy's father, and Callie had felt safe leaving her roommate in Brad's hands while she came home for some much needed rest. Brad had promised to bring Tandy home just as soon as visiting hours were over, and until then all Callie wanted was a hot bath and a few hours of solitude.

It had begun to rain lightly on the way home and Callie had not had a coat. She was damp and uncomfortable, and even her bones ached. She could not decide which she was most in need of: the bath or something hot to drink.

The horror of the past few days penetrated her very soul, like a stain she could not get clean or an odor that clung to every pore. Every time she closed her eyes, the scene replayed in her head, the boy, the gun, the explosion. . . and every time it did, the pressure that built in her chest was like the probing of a fresh wound. Was there anything she could have done, something she should have known, something she could have said. . . Questions Callie could not answer and could not avoid much longer.

She automatically flipped on the television set on her way to the kitchen. The newscaster's voice reached her over the sound of running water as she filled the teapot. "Senator Jonathan Stevens is pronounced in satisfactory condition today after an attempt on his life yesterday afternoon. The radical group called the Red Knights claim responsibility for the assassination attempt on the conservative Democrat from Ohio, and the man arrested for the attempt, Ralph Overson, professes to be a member of that group acting on orders. According to government sources, the Red Knights have threatened further retaliation unless Overson is released. . ."

Callie switched off the television set, her teeth on edge, and then the phone rang.

"If you hadn't answered this time," Jerry said angrily, "I was going to be on the next flight out. Don't you know I've been worried out of my mind about you?"

Callie sank tiredly to the chair beside the telephone. "I'm okay, Jerry," she said. "It's just been—kind of hectic around here lately." It was hard to even make her mind focus. She did not want to talk to Jerry. She didn't want to think. She only wanted to close her eyes and sink into oblivion, but she knew that would never happen. She also knew there were things she should tell Jerry as a reporter and a friend, but at the moment all of them eluded her. And the only thing Callie could think to ask was, "If they know the Red Knights are responsible for the shooting, why doesn't someone do something?"

"A minor point of the law, love," replied Jerry. "You can only try a man for conspiracy if there's evidence to prove it. I don't think the police even know who the rest of these jokers are." And then his voice gentled. "You don't sound very okay."

Callie took a breath. "I know. It's just—hard."

"Yeah, it's different reading about it in the papers. You were pretty close to it this time, weren't you?"

Jerry did not know how close she had been.

"Look," he said after a moment, "I know this is probably not the best time, but I tried to call you before—well, before all this happened. And I wanted you to hear it from me before it hits the papers. It's not going to help you much, but we've found the link between Jed Frye and the Red Knights."

And something within Callie quickened. It was over, she kept telling herself, it was all over. She had seen the worst of her father and of men like him, and she did not want to know anymore, she did not want to get any more involved... But it was her voice that said into the telephone, "Tell me."

Jerry took a breath. "The reason this didn't come out before was because the amounts were so small, and it took a long time to trace them. And then some of the banks involved were reluctant, for security reasons, to admit they'd been the victims of computer theft..."

Everything within Callie grew very still.

"The only way we made the connection at all was because the thieves got a little cocky and started leaving a sign on the computer program...a cartoon character. That's not uncommon; it happens all the time with computer break-ins—it's their way of showing you that they're smarter than the computer. But here's the thing, Callie. Do you remember when Frye did his bank jobs how one of his men would always spray paint on the side of the building—"

"Kilroy was here," Callie said dully.

"And guess what the computer character was that the hackers left on the program? It's not solid evidence at all, and it doesn't prove anything, but if eventually the funds that have been stolen can be traced back to the Red Knights and Jed Frye..."

Brad, Callie thought, and the receiver slipped from her fingers.

Brad.

Brad, who couldn't resist showing off his expertise on the computer to impress an older woman... "Banks are the easiest systems in the world to break into..." Brad, who could afford his own computer terminal and a sparkling new Trans Am; Brad, who ran the program on both Sage McCormick and Jed Frye; Brad, who had *invited Callie to that party*...

And it echoed in her brain, "... the Red Knights threaten further retaliation unless Overson is released..."

Brad, who was at this moment waiting at the hospital to drive Tandy home.

Callie did not remember hanging up the phone. Tandy's lavender raincoat was the only thing she could find to protect herself from the elements, so Callie pulled it on, tightening the hood over her head as she ran out into the night.

Rain was coming down in streaks that looked like shards of glass against the shallow relief of streetlights. For a moment Callie hesitated in the shadows of the building. She knew she was acting on impulse, not logic, and that she should take her time and think this thing through carefully, but something within her—an instinct of danger stronger than anything she had ever felt before—pushed her on. And all she could think of was that Tandy was now in the hands of one of the men who had tried to kill her father and she had to warn her...

Callie heard the movement before she felt the clutch of an iron arm around her throat. She tried to scream but nothing escaped the pressure of that arm, not even breath. And it all happened so fast, in a matter of seconds... She struggled and felt someone else grab her arm. Her heel made contact with a hard shin and she heard a surprised grunt. She saw dark figures around her, twisting and pulling her, and she struggled as she was half lifted and half turned, the sound of her fight for breath like a high mewing in her ears. And then, surprised eyes behind a dark ski mask. Someone swore violently, and the vise that gripped her arms and her neck loosened just a fraction—just enough for her to kick out violently, and then Callie was free.

She was running, stumbling, and gasping, but she knew she hadn't a chance because already she could hear pursuing footsteps and panting breath, and then there was a shout, "Let her go, you fool! It's the wrong girl!"

The wrong girl! It echoed and re-echoed in her mind over the scratching sounds of her frantic running feet, and the night and the rain swirled into hysteria as she had a clear vision of Tandy in her bright lavender raincoat that was known all over campus... Callie had not been wrong. Tandy was in danger...they wanted Tandy... They wanted Tandy, but they had mistaken Callie for her... She had to run. She had to warn her.

Callie did not realize that this final shock had put her over the edge of hysteria induced by stress and exhaustion. She did not know where she was running, what she was going to do, whom she was trying to find. She only knew that she had to keep moving...

The rain had slowed to a cold, misty drizzle that blurred the world into a kaleidoscope of shadows and tears. Callie's weary legs could not keep running, her lungs were bursting with exertion, and every stab of cold air was like a knife in her chest. She could hear the echo of her heartbeat and the gasping sobs that dragged oxygen into her throat. She was so tired. She only wanted to go home.

The fog-shrouded street was empty and silent except for the lonely scrape of Callie's footsteps against the pavement. Her muscles ached, her mind was dull, she was exhausted. But she had to keep moving, just a few more steps would bring her to safety, just here, just up the road...just there where windows glowed with yellow warmth and woodsmoke curled from the chimney...just a few more steps would bring her home.

Her cramping legs took her up the three stone steps, and she lifted her fist and brought it down weakly on the heavy oak door. The door that stood between her and a safe haven, the door that would keep all danger out...

And Callie sobbed out loud in relief as that door slowly swung open and on its threshold stood a welcoming figure, bathed in golden light... Callie stumbled weakly into the strong arms of Sage McCormick.

He was real, he was solid, he was holding her, soothing her. And she was sobbing incoherently and clinging to him, her words desperate and broken, "Help me—hold me...Tandy—they're trying to get Tandy. They thought I was her. They're going to hurt her...Sage, help me; don't let—"

And then Callie lifted her face; through tear-streaked vision his face swam into view and she froze. For behind Sage was a long-haired, bearded man in a battered sombrero. His corded arm restrained a pale and terrified Tandy, and he held a gun pointed directly at Callie.

Chapter Thirteen

Callie wished for the first time in her life for the weakness to faint. That scene would be etched forever on her mind: the warmth of Sage's body against hers, the faint fan of his breath across her wet cheek, the strength of his arms. The scent of logs crackling in the fireplace. The glow of yellow lamplight. And the hard-eyed man who held Tandy prisoner and Callie at gunpoint.

And then suddenly Tandy broke free. Running, she flung herself upon Callie, sobbing out unintelligible half sentences and broken phrases. Sage barked, "For God's sake, Axom, put that thing away! Can't you see they've both been through enough without your scaring them to death?"

The man in the sombrero carefully lowered the gun, but he did not take his hard, mistrustful eyes off Callie, as he came cautiously over to her. Callie tightened her arms around Tandy, though whether it was to protect herself or the hysterical girl she did not know, and then Sage gently took her shoulders. "Callie," he said quietly, soothingly, "this is

George Axom, special agent with the FBI. You don't have to be afraid of him. You're safe here.''

And then Callie was sitting on the sofa, wrapped in the red-and-blue afghan. Sage was pressing into her hand a glass with a small measure of amber liquid in it, and Tandy was kneeling beside her, alternately wiping tears of shock and relief and chattering, "He—he came for me at the hospital. The—agents that were guarding my father, they let him take me. I was s-so scared. H-he said...that s-someone was planning to kidnap me and that I w-would be safe here..."

Sage glanced at her. "You have your friend Brad to thank for that," he said. "He found out the plan and couldn't go through with it...so he came to me." And he urged the glass gently to Callie's lips. "Come on, drink. You're going to be all right."

Callie took one sip but the warm liquid did nothing to ease the cottony web that numbed her brain. She stared at Sage and at Tandy and at the evil-looking man behind her... Then Sage glanced over his shoulder. "Take Tandy to the kitchen and see if you can't get her calmed down, George," he said quietly. "This place is going to be crawling with agents in a few minutes, and there'll be a lot of questions..." And to Tandy, he smiled. "Go with him, okay? Just hang in there for a little while longer... I promise you, this nightmare is going to be over."

Tandy, apparently made of much stronger stuff than Callie had ever suspected, took one look at Callie's pale drawn face, sniffled a last time, and rose without protest to go with George. But not until Sage moved onto the sofa and gathered her in his arms did the nightmare really start to end for Callie.

For a long time he simply held her, imparting strength through silence, comfort through his embrace. Callie knew only one thing and that simple fact she knew quite clearly: she had run to Sage in time of trouble, and he had been here for her. She knew that whatever he told her she would accept. But she was glad that, at last, it was the truth.

"George and I," he began at length, quietly, "have been assigned to this Red Knights case for the past year. . . soon after we began to suspect they might be gathering enough force to be a real threat to domestic—and possibly even international— peace. A small group with no funding, you see, didn't rate much more than a low place on the list of subversive organizations, but when they started tapping banks through computers and slowly accumulating enough to buy weapons. . ."

Callie blinked at him, dazed. As hard as she tried, she could not understand. Maybe it was the brandy. Maybe it was the warmth of Sage's presence, his mesmerizing touch. He smiled at her. "Poor darling," he said. "This doesn't make much sense to you, does it? Believe me, I can't say that it makes a whole lot of sense to me either. . ." And he sighed, dropping his eyes. "I joined the military right after college," he explained, "for all the noble, idealistic and utterly wrong reasons—honor and glory, victory and applause. . . I got assigned to Intelligence, and the things I saw, the things I did, were neither honorable nor glorious, and the last thing I wanted was applause for them. Hell," he said, and for just a moment there was that familiar twist of bitterness to his tone as she felt his muscles tighten, "I was nothing more than a spy. I called the shots when there was no clear line between right and wrong; I made decisions that cost hundreds of innocent people their lives... I wormed my way into the confidence of simple men, and then I betrayed them. I saw enough bureaucratic bungling and diplomatic tongue-twisting to turn my stomach, and even when I knew right from wrong, my hands were tied. I guess I wanted to change the world," he reflected quietly, "but I realized it wasn't mine for the changing..."

And slowly Callie began to understand. She lay against the quiet, steady beating of his heart and felt his warmth begin to seep into her, and so many things about Sage became clear. Not a traitor at all, but a patriot without a cause. He had seen the horror of invasion and resistance; he had participated for his country's sake in that rebellion and found himself powerless to stop it. He had come away scarred and disillusioned. He had done wrong things for right reasons, and under orders... And Callie wondered, along with Sage, if there ever were any right reasons for something like that.

"So," he said abruptly, closing the door on a story that Callie knew instinctively would take years to tell, "I got out. Only with a security clearance like mine, you never really get out... And when it became known that a terrorist group was gaining power on this very campus, my talents were once again needed by my country...and I got volunteered.'' And again there was that bitter twist to his lips. Callie wondered if there would ever be anything she could do to keep that expression from returning to his face. She only hoped that, through the years, she would have the chance to try...

And she said, slowly grasping, ''That's why your file was deleted from the computer.''

He looked at her surprised, and then a little rueful. ''So. You got that far, did you?'' He nodded. ''Obviously since the computer was the link to the whole thing, we couldn't have someone accidentally stumbling over my full dossier, so we put a protect code on it...just like we did with Jed Frye.''

And now Callie's attention quickened. ''Then...'' the words came out in a lump of dread. ''It was him, all along, who was behind this...''

Very gently, Sage bent and brushed her damp hair with a kiss. ''No, honey. Jed Frye was just a code name that I used to log the case. The only connection the real man had with any of it was that the way these guys were operating reminded me of some of Frye's early escapades...like leaving the Kilroy code on the bank thefts. It wasn't such an unusual coincidence... Frye's story is pretty well known. These guys were just modeling themselves after a legend.''

So her father had had nothing to do with it after all. Nothing lived of him at this campus but his legend... It had all been another wild goose chase.

And the relief that slowly spread through Callie was headier than the brandy, surprising, welcome, confusing... And other things were pressing her. Jed Frye was in her past. The man in whose arms she rested was her present, and it was that which concerned her now.

She looked up at him, her eyes lightening and darkening with wonder and adjustment as she tried to absorb and make sense of it all. "So," she said carefully, "you were infiltrating the Red Knights..."

He nodded soberly. "It wasn't an easy job either. These guys were smart and very careful. I was just starting to get in tight with Overson—he was the leader...but apparently not tight enough." The lines around his mouth tightened grimly. "I didn't have the first idea about what they planned for Stevens. None of us did. Just one more battle we lost..."

Callie touched his cheek lightly, wanting to smooth away the pain, the disillusionment, the sense of failure that was etched so harshly upon his face. "Sage," she said softly, "why didn't you tell me?"

It was an effort for him to smile. "How could I?" he asked simply. "You were my prime suspect." And then his eyes slowly closed, his breath was long and heavy as he tightened his arms around her, drawing her to him as though afraid she might at any moment slip through his fingers. "Oh, Callie," he said lowly, "you don't know what you put me through. Everything you said, everything you did, pointed to the fact that you were a top candidate for membership in the organization. . . if you weren't already a part of it. We'd nailed Brad Johnson months ago as the computer expert, and you hadn't been here two days before you were tight with him. You were stealing computer time like it was going out of style and you knew Jed Frye. . . I should have been down on you with all four barrels. Your showing up when you did was tantamount to flashing a neon billboard across the campus that said Danger, Danger. . . I knew it. I saw it. All the evidence was there. . . and I ignored it. And worse still, I knew that I was ignoring it and putting my life and who knew who else's on the line because I wanted to believe you. Because," he said simply, "I loved you."

And that, after all, was the key.

Through the night, as government agents interviewed both Callie and Tandy, Callie began to gradually put the story together. Brad, the one person Callie had ignored in her own efforts to try to get at the truth, had been the centrifugal force around whom all the entire drama revolved. Shortly after he had run the program that revealed the link between Jed Frye and Sage McCormick, he had done some exploring on his own and come up with an accurate guess as to Sage's real identity. The crisis Brad had faced in the ensuing weeks and the choices he had made were something that only Brad himself could explain. He had not tipped off any of the others about the spy in their midst. Perhaps it was because he was beginning to see how dangerous what they were doing really was. Perhaps it was because, since meeting Tandy, he was beginning to look for a way out and was holding Sage as a reserve escape clause. Perhaps it was merely that, deep down, Brad was just as Callie had first thought—a niçe boy. He had not known about the plot to assassinate Senator Stevens until after the fact...apparently only a small circle of top members knew that plan. Security within the organization was, indeed, very tight. But when the plan to kidnap Tandy and hold her against Overson's release was revealed, Brad had made the right choice. He had gone to Sage and told him the whole story, in plenty of time for Tandy to be brought to safety. No one could have guessed that Callie, flying from the house in a panic, would be mistaken for her roommate. Callie shuddered when she realized that, had Brad been a different kind of person or had he made a different choice, she could have been the reason Sage's cover was blown—and could have possibly cost him his life. Brad was now being held in police custody with a promise of plea bargaining for turning state's evidence and agreeing to identify the other members of the organization. The nightmare, at long last, was over for all of them.

Tandy was being taken to a place she could be more adequately protected until all of the members of the oganization were taken into custody, and security was being tightened around the hospital. At three o'clock in the morning they all left, closing the door on the harshness and the corruption of the outside world, leaving Sage and Callie alone, and together.

"Will Tandy be all right?" Callie worried, standing at the window in the shelter of Sage's arm, watching the taillights of the last car disappear into the mist. "I mean, she's in no danger now, is she? The worst of it is over?"

Sage tenderly stroked Callie's hair away from her eyes, and his smile was vague. "Yes," he said. "The worst of it is over...for this time and this campus."

She looked at him, and she saw reflected in his eyes the pain for other times, other places, past and present...the sorrow of knowing that one man really could not change the world, no matter how hard he tried.

"You made a difference this time, Sage," Callie said softly. Her hand lightly stroked his neck, tracing the collarbone, caressing the warmth and softness of smooth flesh. And gradually she saw the lines of stress upon his face ease.

He looked down at her. The pain was gone from his eyes, in its stead was a deep and certain contentment. "Yes," he agreed. "This time it was worth it. And I think," he added quietly, "together, you and I can go on making a difference...in small ways, in little things, one day at a time. Maybe that's the only way worlds are ever changed."

Callie smiled at him and slipped her arms around his neck. "Hold me, Sage," she said.

He did.

Chapter Fourteen

Three weeks had passed, and time, by its very nature, has a way of restoring normalcy to even the most chaotic of scenes. The campus was back to its usual routine after what seemed an almost anticlimactic flurry of excitement when the story of the Red Knights and the computer theft broke. Tandy and her father had flown back to Washington, where Senator Stevens was recuperating rapidly under the loving attention of his daughter. Callie's latest letter from her ex-roommate indicated that, harsh as it may have been, the brush with death had brought both father and daughter to a deeper understanding and a closeness they had never before shared. In that way the rewards were worth the cost.

Members of the Red Knights had been identified by Brad and were awaiting trials on everything from conspiracy to grand larceny. Brad himself stood a good chance of facing only a light sentence in a minimum security facility. He had been more than cooperative with the officials and confessed nothing but a relief that it was over, and he was out of it. Even Sage agreed that the boy had probably never considered it as anything more than a lark until the assassination attempt, and the pure horror of that was probably all the rehabilitation he needed. Sage even joked that when Brad got out, he would probably make a fortune designing video games.

Winter's approaching winds had swept away most of the autumn leaves, and the afternoon sun did little to warm a bitter cold as Callie and Sage walked home from class. The campus crowd was thinning out; no one lingered on the benches or picnicked on the grass but walked purposefully from one building to another, pausing only long enough to call a greeting or engage in a brief conversation. Soon they would be hurrying across snow-encrusted lawns, their collars turned to the wind, looking neither right nor left...such were the changing seasons.

Callie had changed her major from Mideastern Affairs to Education and was settling into the new class load quite easily. It had been an easy decision to make, and she did not understand why she had not thought of it before. If her only desire in changing careers had been to be the person molding policy instead of just interpreting it, what better choice than teaching? And there was a very excellent possibility that when her course credit was completed, there would be a place for her here, in the Languages Department of the university. She couldn't ask for more.

The horror was fading, the mystery was gone.

The episode could be relegated to their past, not forgotten but no longer a threat...except for one thing.

Sage and Callie walked with their arms linked, their hands entwined and warmed in one of the pockets of Sage's coat. The sun felt good on Callie's face, and they did not hurry, enjoying the outdoors despite the cold. And Callie said, "Sage... do you remember that morning that I asked you about Jed Frye?" She glanced up at him, and there was no evasion in his eyes. There was no room for secrets between them any longer. He nodded. "I asked if he was on this campus and if you knew him... You didn't answer, but I saw it in your eyes. He is here, isn't he?"

Callie felt Sage's fingers tighten on hers within the warmth of his flannel-lined pocket. And he nodded.

Her heart speeded once, then calmed to its normal rhythm. "And you know who he is?"

"I've known for about three years now," was his simple reply.

Callie stopped and turned to him. There was hope in her eyes, but no desperation. "Will you tell me," she asked quietly, "who he is?"

Sage's eyes slowly left hers and traveled silently across the campus. Hesitantly Callie followed the direction of his gaze until it rested at last on a figure crossing the lawn a few yards before them. A man in an unkempt overcoat and flying silver hair who battled a gust of wind for the custody of a sheaf of papers he was carrying... A man with the kindest eyes she had ever seen. Sea-faring eyes, gray eyes, like her own...

"Professor Chalmers," she whispered.

Sage looked at her gravely. "He's made his escape, Callie. He's repaying his debt to society in his own way. He's been here for twelve years and the research he's doing has already contributed to advances in medicine... I'm not even sure he remembers he used to be Jed Frye anymore. Are you going to tell him?" he queried gently. "Are you going to tell him he's been found?"

Callie looked back across the lawn. The wind had succeeded in wrestling one of his papers from him, and he made a comical sight chasing it down. Professor Chalmers, a harmless old man who had dedicated his life to science, the butt of campus jokes...not Jed Frye. Not a man on the run, not a fugitive from justice, not even a man who once had unknowingly fathered a daughter...

"No," Callie whispered, and unexpectedly her eyes misted with tears. But she was smiling as she looked back at Sage. "I'm not going to tell him."

The slow light in his eyes registered approval, pride, and admiration for her decision. He slipped his arm around her waist and gave her a brief hug as they started walking again. And then suddenly he stopped. "I almost forgot." Sage removed his arm and dug into his jean pocket for something. "I had this made for you today. Now I won't have to worry about you being locked out when we don't get home at the same time." And in her hand he placed a shiny new house key.

Callie looked at it for a moment, and the emotions that swelled up within her over so simple a gift choked her speech, precluded all but the joy and the wonder that shone in her eyes as she looked up at him. "It's your house, too," Sage reminded her gently, and she stepped mutely into his arms. He kissed her.

The breeze rattled the limbs overhead, and the last of autumn's golden leaves swirled down upon them like a benediction. Then they turned and, arm and arm, walked the rest of the way home.

Harlequin Photo
~ Calendar ~

Turn Your Favorite Photo into a Calendar.

Uniquely yours, this 10x17½" calendar features your favorite photograph, with any name you wish in attractive lettering at the bottom. A delightfully personal and practical idea!

Send us your favorite color print, black-and-white print, negative, or slide, any size (we'll return it), along with **3** proofs of purchase (coupon below) from a June or July release of Harlequin Romance, Harlequin Presents, Harlequin Superromance, Harlequin American Romance or Harlequin Temptation, plus $5.75 (includes shipping and handling).

JULY 1984

The Browns

Introducing...

Harlequin Intrigue

A wonderful opportunity to collect the brand-new titles in this adventurous and compelling series.

Don't delay! Complete and mail this coupon TODAY while quantities last.